... a fasci......... .... *is written with a remarkable dose of sensitivity to human nature. The life stories are so real they could be genuine characters presenting the important ethical but also human questions that arise in transplantation ... a lot more thorough, authentic and enjoyable than any bioethical textbook on transplanta...*
SCOTTISH COUNC... MAN BIOETHICS

In a page-turner of a novel ... Hazel McHaffie maps out the moral maze surrounding organ donation with clear-headed compassion. Confronting and encapsulating the related issues, medical, ethical, social and emotional, she tells a story which is gripping in itself and valuable in its focus on a subject which, in the widest sense, affects us all.
CORNFLOWER BOOKS

There are very few novels which deal with the issues of contemporary medical ethics in the lively and intensely readable way which Hazel McHaffie's books do.
ALEXANDER McCALL SMITH

... well written and researched ... presents issues of medicine, law and ethics in a very human and readily understood manner.
BRITISH MEDICAL ASSOCIATION

You are gripped from the very beginning, but as you turn the pages, you are compelled to think about the issues. It is an excellent formula.
BARONESS MARY WARNOCK

McHaffie has honed the formula for engaging with ethical issues in the narrative of her novels, particularly through her talent for telling the story from different perspectives and adding an element of mystery which makes her novels hard to put down.
INSTITUTE OF MEDICAL ETHICS

Gripping and thoughtful. Hazel McHaffie writes about ethical issues in medicine with empathy and real emotional truth and power; revealing the impact of difficult decisions on the professionals, patients and relatives involved, and making you care about the characters. Over My Dead Body is a another page-turner, with surprising twists and family secrets making it hard to put down. Evocative and engaging, her novels deserve to be widely read.
RACHEL WARREN (formerly sessional ethics tutor, King's College, London School of Medicine)

HAZEL McHAFFIE trained as a nurse and midwife, gained a PhD in Social Sciences and was Deputy Director of Research in the Institute of Medical Ethics. She is the author of almost a hundred published articles and books, and won the British Medical Association Book of the Year Award in 2002. *Right to Die* was shortlisted for the BMA Popular Medicine prize in 2008. *Over My Dead Body* is her eighth published novel set in the world of medical ethics.

OVER MY DEAD BODY

HAZEL McHAFFIE

First published 2013

ISBN: 978-0-9926231-0-4

British Library Cataloguing in Publication Data. A catalogue record for this book is available from the British Library.

The paper used in this book is recyclable. It is made from low chlorine pulps produced in a low energy, low emissions manner from renewable forests.

Published by VelvetEthics Press
12 Mayburn Terrace, Loanhead, Scotland EH20 9EJ

Printed by Bell & Bain Ltd, Glasgow

Acknowledgements

I owe a specially warm debt of gratitude to Deborah MacDonald, Kate MacDonald, Karen Nicolson, Mary Sweeney and Gordon Brown who so generously shared their firsthand personal experience of organ donation with me, the emotions as well as the facts, and so much more besides.

Lesley Logan not only gave me the benefit of her extensive knowledge as a professional in the world of organ donation but also kindly read an early manuscript with an eagle eye for anomalies in my understanding.

Katherine Kirsop and 'Martin' kept me right on police procedure and terminology and saved me from showing my age.

Libby MacRae, Monica Thompson and Margaret McGhee checked the accents, dialect and idioms which I appropriated from their native areas.

Rosalyn Crich, Jonathan McHaffie, Patricia McClure, Christine Windmill, Helen Balsillie, Katharine Crichton, Kerry Barker, Anne Vann, Roslyn Edwards and Hilary Amyes all gave me superb feedback during the writing process and have been instrumental in improving the quality of the finished product. David McHaffie did his usual rigorous check for typographical errors.

Tom Bee has worked his special magic on the cover. Linda Gillard gave me the benefit of her extensive experience of the publishing process.

To them all I say a huge thank you; I hope you can feel happy to be associated with this novel. If not, the blame is all mine.

PROLOGUE

Carole

OH NO! HE'S BACK.

    His calling card this time is tiny, the dark green and purple barely visible in the shadow of the granite stone. A simple posy of violets. No ribbon, no message. Even so, the bile of fear rises in the back of my throat and I freeze on the spot.

    Last time it was pale pink rosebuds, a bright patch in the gloom. I left them to fade to paper brown, then murky slime when it rained, in case whoever brought them came back, or was watching.

    Who is it, taunting me? I know where she is. I know everything about your family. I know what happened. I know.

    These violets are fresh, delivered today, I shouldn't wonder. Did I interrupt a private vigil? Or is this the next move in a slow game to rattle me?

    I sneak a look around me but there's not a single living soul in the cemetery at this hour. I bend to smell them, not touching, just savouring. The wave of memories hits me in the gut and I close my eyes against the familiar pain. Why didn't I think of this?

    'Violets,' I whisper. 'Your favourite.'

    Whoever it is knows that.

    'Symbolic of faithfulness,' a florist once told me. 'You won't get them this time of year, but white carnations say the same thing.'

    White carnations? I don't think so!

I kneel beside the gently rounded mound for a moment, thinking, remembering, in silence. It's still damp with morning dew. I fold a plastic bag several times into a cushion for my knees. No point in inviting a flare up of my arthritis, although now ...

I rake the soft soil briskly, snip off four damaged leaves from the rose bush, and run a polishing cloth over the stone. There, good as new again.

'OK, I know, I know. You wouldn't care. But I do.'

Turning sideways to sit more comfortably my arm brushes against the hardness in my right breast.

'I've got two things to tell you today. I'm saying that up front to make sure I don't chicken out this time. First, the lump. I found it three weeks before ... before the accident. I realised straight away, of course, I'm not stupid, but I didn't want Guy to know, didn't want him feeling obliged to look after me. It could wait till I was on my own, I thought. Then we lost you, and ever since I've been so busy being mother and father and sister and playmate and counsellor and everything else, there simply wasn't time to bother about it. And now it's too late. They told me yesterday. It's in my liver, lungs, bones. But don't fret, my darling, I'm OK. They've promised me plenty of pain relief.

'I don't know what there is beyond this life. They tell you the best is yet to come, don't they? Oh, they promised me so many amazing things for you that I came to wonder why anyone went on living here in the present. But they can't all be right. I hope there's something afterwards though, and that you'll be there. I think of that when the pain's bad in the middle of the night. Every day, every hour, every minute, one step nearer to you.'

Out of the corner of my eye I see the windmills twirling in the breeze. Twelve plots for twelve children – twelve little Maddies – half of them covered with toys all year round (testament to the fact that plastic doesn't disintegrate, it only fades), half untended.

'How you'd hate all that paraphernalia! Elaborate headstones, angels, cherubs, verses and quotations: God only chooses the best ... Gone to be a sunbeam ... Too good for this

world. *There's one though, that touches me every time I see it: Kiera Anita Winters. 14.2.2001. A Valentine's Day baby. A single day; a lifetime of sadness. At least we have proper memories to keep you alive in our hearts.*

'We kept it simple for you too, just names and dates, nothing more. Didn't want anyone finding it, desecrating it. We who loved – love – you, know where you are, and it doesn't matter what anybody else knows or thinks. You'd have pooh-poohed any kind of stone probably, but I was so terribly afraid that one day I'd forget where you were. I needed something, *just in case. That was before I knew I'm not going to be around long enough to get dementia.*

'Oliver thought you'd probably prefer a field of wild flowers somewhere, with a tree maybe to mark the spot, but the nearest one is on the other side of town. I couldn't see how I'd travel so far through city traffic every day, not with my new responsibilities. So this plot, right on the edge, close to the hedge, where nobody comes except to visit you, was our compromise.

'It's daft, I know, thinking something dire will happen if I don't come to visit you. The worst thing imaginable has already happened. Three times now – four, if you count Drew. Superstitious nonsense, you'd scoff. I know. But remember how you felt if you accidentally stepped on a crack in the pavement? That elaborate ritual ... I seriously worried about your mental state, I can tell you, watching you spinning on one foot, whirling your coat above your head, muttering some kind of incantation. And then there was Mr Brownlee's railings; you had to touch every second spiral, remember? And you absolutely couldn't *wear your pink sparkly shoes on Wednesdays. The look you gave me when I told you not to listen to Poppy Winstanley's silly ideas! Well, you'd get your own back now.*

'But coming here, it's much more than superstition. I want to come. I have to come. Because you're here. I want to be close to you, talk to you, about everything.

'Oh but, darling, it breaks my heart every time. Being here makes it all too real. And more than that, it reminds me of another grave that I don't visit. And that's the second thing

I have to tell you about. Sally. We kept it from you back then, when it happened. The doctors, the police, the social people, everybody agreed: no point in blighting your life at such a young age. That's why we moved right away where nobody knew us. Even so, I dreaded you finding out somehow.

'I thought I'd put it behind me, but no. One of the policemen we saw after the accident, he found out, so if he did, other people might. This person who comes to your grave, brings flowers ...

'Who knows what they might do – to you, to any of us?

'Was I right not to tell you? Sometimes I wondered if you guessed things simply didn't add up. But you have to believe me, it was to protect you. Now though, it's different. I'm facing my own end, I need to clear my conscience.

'Besides, the truth can't hurt you any more.'

PART 1

Chapter 1

Elvira

ELVIRA THREW THE CUSHION with a muffled squawk.

'Give me strength, Oliver Reynolds! Are you out of the *ark*?'

'It's true,' Oliver protested, ducking too late. 'Every man I know wants a Nigella-look-alike waiting at home.'

'Well, course they do,' she scoffed, miming voluptuous.

'Cooking his meals, I'm talking about.'

'Yeah, yeah, yeah! And the rest.'

'Busy working men, kids, families, they need proper nourishment.'

'That's what Sainsbury's and Tesco are for.'

'*Proper* meals. Home cooking, I mean.'

'So do I. From the supermarket to the microwave to the table.'

Oliver neatly fielded the second missile. 'Blimey, Ellie. You don't believe in cooking. You don't believe in ironing. You don't believe in housework. What *do* you believe in?'

'Freedom from slavery. Emancipation. Ever heard of it?'

'Is cooking for your *family* slavery?'

'If I don't choose to do it.'

Oliver stared at her, eyes narrowing. 'So who made that lasagne yesterday?'

'Willow. With a little help from her grandmother.'

'*Willow*? But she's only ...'

'Nine, going on forty-nine. I know, I know. I gave birth to her, remember? I do know how old she is.'

'So if that isn't child slavery ...'

Elvira flung herself back onto the bed, hands lifted in despair. She looked fabulous, her red hair flaring out across the cream duvet, her hazel eyes wide with the intensity of her point.

'Willow *wants* to do it. She *likes* cooking. She *chooses* to do it. That's the difference.'

'Whereas your mind is on higher things,' he said, letting his eyes deliberately wander.

'I'm not sure about *higher*,' she giggled, uncurling her body slowly, watching his face. 'And in your case it's definitely lower.'

He grinned.

'Well, if you will wear such skimpy skirts ... and have such fantastic legs.'

The bed sagged as he knelt on the edge and leaned towards her. She reached up to pull him close. Neither heard the door open.

'*Muuuuummy!*' Willow's eyes were blazing, her thin body, poured into blue Lycra, taut with rage. 'You *said*! You *promised*,' she hissed.

'Yoiks!' Elvira scrambled off the bed. 'It's OK, honey, I'm coming.'

'I *hate* being late. You *know* I hate being late.'

'We won't be. I was only giving Maddie a few more minutes. I'll wake her now and we'll be off. Promise.'

Willow glared at Oliver and flounced out of the room. Elvira followed, slicing her hand across her throat as she went.

Oliver lay still, listening to the sounds of conflicted motherhood.

Elvira's soft, 'Maddie. Time to wake up, sweetheart.'

Willow's persistent, 'You promised. You *promised*.'

'We won't be late, Willow. Don't worry.'

'Why doesn't *he* look after Maddie, so we could go right now?'

'Because Oliver has other things to do. Besides Maddie likes being with her big sister. She wants to go to dancing classes just like you when she grows up.'

'You never *used* to be late for everything.'

'Willow, we won't be late. Come on, Maddie, arms in, there's a good girl.'

'Mrs Whittock *told* us not to be late today. I *told* you she said that. There's somebody important coming, *specially,* to watch us.'

'I know, honey, I know. There we go, Maddie, all ready. Don't you look pretty?'

'I wish I could go to boarding school.'

Oliver gritted his teeth. How did Ellie manage not to throttle the kid?

'How about you go downstairs, Willow, and get your coat. I'll just pop to the loo and be down. Two seconds, max.'

Oliver could almost feel the daggered look that would have greeted this further delay. He slid off the bed and positioned himself so that he could see the landing reflected in the bedroom mirror, ready to pounce when Elvira emerged from the bathroom.

'Oliver, *please!* Not now.' She wrenched herself out of his grasp.

'Slave!' he taunted, grinning at her.

'It's all your fault.'

'I'll do penance tonight. Promise. Might even cook for the demon Willow.'

'It'll take more than chicken and chips to win her over this time.'

And she was gone.

Oliver watched the bright red Fiat Punto vanish from sight. He sighed. She was everything he wanted. Well, almost.

Silence filled the car.

Elvira glanced in the mirror. Willow glowered. Maddie, vaguely aware of the atmosphere, found solace in her thumb and sucked rhythmically, her long eyelashes drooping occasionally, startling awake again as if she feared the repercussions if she dozed off in the middle of the storm.

Twelve minutes. Twelve measly minutes.

She accelerated past an ancient Ford driven by a man surely too old and decrepit to be on the road, pulling in in the nick of time as the local bus appeared. An empty Coke can lurched to the front and back again.

'Nothing's the same since *he* came,' Willow muttered.

'Look, darling, I know you miss Daddy. So do I. But he's not coming back, and I can't do anything to change that.'

'We don't have to have *him* instead.'

'He's not "instead". But I like Oliver, he's been very kind to us, so, please, try not to be so mean to him.'

'It's not *me* that's mean. *I'm* not the one who makes people late when they don't want to be. It's not *me* that doesn't want to do things with me and Maddie any more.'

'Oh, that's not true, Willow. I love you girls, more than anything else in the world. You know I do.'

The driver of a gleaming BMW blared his horn as he flashed past. Ellie gripped the steering wheel more tightly. All right for him, on his own, in a brand new powerful car, free to go whatever speed he chose, overtake when he chose, speak when he chose, even listen to music if he chose. He didn't have eight ... no, seven shrinking minutes to get to Mrs Whittock's dancing class.

She'd taken the corner hundreds of times before. It was on her daily route between home and school, she'd grown up less than ten miles from it, and she'd practised the optimal speed for negotiating it smoothly on umpteen occasions before her driving test. But this was the first time she'd driven towards it at thirty-eight miles an hour, with a skim of water under her nearside wheels, and the muddy tyre tracks from Billy Menzies' tractor on her other side, with Willow saying, 'Mrs Whittock said ...', and the baby suddenly vomiting, at the same time as an articulated lorry drove towards them at precisely thirty-three miles an hour, diverted from his usual route taking a truck-load of provisions to Sainsbury's at Straiton where Ellie shopped for her family every Friday.

Chapter 2

Willow

I SHUT MY EYES, pretend we're already there.

Mrs Whittock's smiling, saying, 'You look lovely, Willow. Perfect.'

I haven't got to think about being late, or Mrs Whittock being cross, or even missing my chance to dance for the lady who's coming specially. She used to be a famous dancer, this lady – whatever her name is. She even danced in front of the Queen once, Mrs Whittock said.

That'll be me one day, in front of the Queen, in one of those lovely white feathery dresses with sparkly bits, and a tiara, and glittery make-up, and right up on my tiptoes. It's not fair. We aren't allowed to do *en pointe* till we're older. Mrs Whittock says eleven or twelve, and you must be ready to practise dancing at least three hours a week. But my friend Jessie, she goes to a different teacher, and her Mrs Callendar lets girls start when they're ten, or *nine* even. I wish *I* could start. I try it at home sometimes but you need proper shoes and everything.

Dancing's my most favouritest thing in the whole world. Better than playtime and PE and art even.

Imagine anybody making me late for *this*! I wish he'd go away to the other side of the world and never come back, ever, ever, *ever*. He's always touching Mummy, and saying silly things that make her giggle. And he really hates me. You can tell. Before it wasn't so bad, he only came once in a while. Mummy was still there for stories and breakfast and packed lunches. But now he keeps coming, and sometimes he's there several *days*. And last Monday she even forgot to say, *'Teeth clean, poppet? Hanky in your pocket?'* She *always* says that.

I haven't told anybody about him, not even Granny. If I ever say his name that means he's real and people will talk about him like he's in our family. He mustn't ever, ever, *ever* be in our family. That's just me and Maddie and Mummy and nobody else.

I sneak a look at her. She's holding the steering wheel really tight. She's *trying* to get me there on time, only she should have left earlier. She *knew* it was important. It's on the calendar in capitals. We *can't* be late.

Crumbs! That man looks cross. Ohhhh. Mummy says you shouldn't ever make that sign. Oliver does it though, when she's not there; I saw him. Mummy wouldn't like him if she knew he did that, I know she wouldn't. Maybe I'll tell her.

Wowweee, this is fast. Like Daddy. Oh I wish Daddy was here now. *He'd* have taken me to dancing tonight. He'd have whistled and said, 'Is this really my little Willow?'

Look at Maddie, she doesn't even know we're late. Must be nice being little like that and not having to worry about anything.

I wish I could go and live with Granny, do cooking all the time, and have sweets, and get to mess about with her paints, and not have to tidy my room. *She'd* make sure I got to Mrs Whittock's on time. And I wouldn't have to see Oliver ever again. And when he was gone I could go back to live with Mummy, and it'd be like it used to be. Only no Daddy.

Why did he have to die? Other people's dads don't die. Nobody else in my class has a dad that died.

Wow, look at all that water.

Oh Maddie! Yuck. Not *today*!

'Mrs Whittock said …'

Chapter 3

Sarah

SARAH SWALLOWED THE remains of her tepid coffee and looked at her watch. The heart should be leaving Theatre 6 about now. Time to check on progress and then go in search of the Mackay parents.

Dougal Alistair was their only son, one month short of his eighteenth birthday. A lanky, freckled lad with spiked blonde hair and an adolescent stubble, who'd brought his mum tea in bed made with cold water when he was five; run away from school when he was eight; finally mastered the difference between *its* and *it's* when he was eleven; won the cross-country run for his house when he was thirteen; dropped all foreign languages from his timetable when he was fourteen; passed his driving test when he was seventeen. His dad was so proud of him he bought a second-hand Citroën at an auction, had it checked and overhauled, and told him: 'It's yours, lad, but mind now, no nonsense. It's a dangerous weapon. You'd never forgive yourself if you knocked somebody down and killed them.' Only he hadn't told Dougal not to kill himself.

The doctor who pronounced life extinct said Dougal wouldn't have known anything about it; he was unconscious at the scene, never regained awareness. But Sarah's imagination couldn't help but conjure up that split second when the lad felt the wheels leave the road, saw the tree approaching at dizzying speed, anticipated the impact.

It was no surprise that his parents wanted to stay in the hospital while the transplant team did their work. Usually the families said their goodbyes and left while the patient was still pink and warm in Intensive Care, but one or other of the Mackays had sat with their boy for every second of every hour since the accident, even through the tests for brain stem death. This day would finally remove the last shred of hope they'd clung to ever since the policeman had come to their door. For the first time Dougal would look dead, feel dead, be indisputably dead. They both had to be there and know for certain. And they had to see for themselves that Sarah had been telling the truth: he wasn't mutilated by the procedure.

She slid the sign to 'Out' under her name: *Sarah Jenkins. Specialist Nurse in Organ Donation.*

The main corridor was empty save for the familiar figure of the chaplain, Ruaidhri Cameron, coming towards her, his fair hair haloed by the fractured sunlight filtering through the glass panels behind him. Sarah smiled, remembering an early conversation when she'd first seen his name badge.

'How on earth d'you pronounce that?'

'It's a Gaelic variant of Rory,' he'd said with a wry grimace. 'Blame my father. My mother wanted to keep it simple; my father reckoned a difficult name would steel his son for the bigger battles in life.'

'Shades of *A Boy Named Sue.*'

'Indeed.'

'So, how *do* you pronounce it?'

'Pretty much the same way – just a couple of rolled rs and a u-a sound here and there. Don't bother with the frills, plain Rory's just fine.'

'No, I like it. It's more musical than Rory. D'you have a second name to fall back on if the going gets tough?'

'No such luck. Ruaidhri Farquhar Emerson. Lethal combination, huh? My father had a sadistic streak. Took me till I was about eleven to write my full name on anything. Mercifully in my day the lads were all called by their surname at school. Cameron suited me just fine.'

Now he gave her a jaunty wave. 'Hi, there. You off body-snatching again?'

She laughed, falling into step beside him. 'Hi, yourself. I might well be second cousin to Burke and Hare, but you seem to have metamorphosed into the angel Gabriel.'

His benign expression changed to one of mock horror. 'Heavens! My father would have a coronary at the very idea. Hardly alpha male material, huh?'

'Just a trick of the light,' she said. 'You look to be in a hurry.'

'ED just paged me. Road traffic collision. Young mum and two kiddies seriously injured. Sounds bad.'

Her groan was heartfelt. 'I hate the ones involving children.'

'Don't we all, but they want me for the grandmother apparently. She's lost the plot. Small wonder, huh?'

Sarah shook her head slowly. 'Poor woman.'

'Well, let's just hope there's no need for *your* services with this one.'

'*The effective, fervent prayer of a righteous man ...*' she quoted. 'I'm off to see the Mackays. They're retrieving the organs as we speak.'

'Best of luck with that one.' He raised one eyebrow. 'Maybe see you later when I'm done with the granny? Exchange notes?'

'That'd be good. I guess we'll both be in need of a hefty caffeine infusion by then.'

He nodded sympathetically. 'Tell the Mackays I'm thinking of them, will you? One brave couple. And page me when you're free.'

'Will do.'

She watched him stride off, not looking back but giving a salute as if he knew she was.

The Mackays were sitting motionless, side by side, hands clenched when she opened the door.

'Is it over?' Dougal's dad croaked. 'Already?'

'Not yet, but everything's going to plan. I only came to see if I could get you anything? Help in any way?'

'I've been thinking ... is it too late to have a say? You know ... about where everything goes?'

Sarah took a quick breath. 'We discussed this,

remember? It's decided by other impartial people, and computers, based on the best match of tissue types, on how ill the potential recipients are, that kind of thing.'

'Give over, Shaun. Not *now*.' His wife nudged him hard with her elbow.

'But it's our ...' And suddenly the control broke. Dougal's dad was sobbing in his wife's arms, her tears dripping unheeded in his greying hair.

Sarah crouched beside them, reaching out from her accumulated wisdom to their pain. A hundred arguments had raced through her brain in that split second: a Labour heart will beat exactly the same in a Conservative body; a black person will see the world in precisely the same way through a white donor's eyes; a Catholic kidney will still cleanse a Protestant body ...

Her voice was gentle. 'I know. I understand. This is desperately hard for you. But you know, what we all have in common is greater than what divides us. And you're giving the gift of life to other really sick people. You're saving other parents, other families, the anguish you're going through right now. Hang on to that.'

He probably didn't register what she was saying, but she had to demonstrate her infinite capacity to be alongside them in their bleak despair. Only ... these days it wasn't infinite. There were times when she had to walk away, times when she felt she'd drown in the tragedies of all these deaths, when the lives saved seemed to be bought at too high a price, when the cost to her too seemed overwhelming.

Losing her boyfriend, Derek, who'd survived living with her erratic schedules and shredded emotions for seventeen months, three weeks and two days, was the latest in a long line of personal sacrifices. She'd missed the call that told her about her father's stroke; she hadn't been there nearly enough for her mother since then; she'd been unable to attend her niece's wedding in Vancouver; she'd forgotten the number of times she'd had to postpone meeting her friends. People only ever pencilled her in nowadays, easily erased.

And the chaplain didn't answer his pager when she rang him, or return her call. Presumably he'd been caught up in some other family's tragedy – that grandmother maybe, or perhaps he too had just been going through the motions.

She downed two mugs of strong coffee. Alone.

By the time she left that night, three hours after Shaun and Gill Mackay said a last goodbye to their teenage son; while Elvira Kennedy's mother was still railing against the injustice of Ruaidhri's God, she was fit only for bed. Alone.

Chapter 4

Carole

I WAS WORKING ON *Elvira's picture when they came, not making much progress, stopping every so often to stretch the shoulder muscles, five times, slowly, rhythmically, just as the osteopath recommended, preventing the aches and pains so I could keep going for longer each day. My mother and aunts were all 'martyrs to arthritis' as they put it, so I'm always trying to delay its takeover bid.*

I'd been tinkering for days. The muted ochre I'd used for the sunlight on the oak leaves was too dull, the perspective in that back row of cottages somehow didn't ring true, the shadow from the central tree was too dominant, the figure in the doorway too indistinct ...

It was a gamble, I know, giving my own artwork to my critical daughter, but I had a special reason for making an extra effort this year. It was more than: Happy thirty-sixth birthday. It was: I love you; forgive me for what I'm about to do.

Insecurity was the last thing Ellie needed. She'd only recently started to believe in her own talent, thanks to a letter from Enitharmon Press, the forty-ninth publisher she'd approached: We're most interested in your first volume of poems.

My daughter, almost a published poet! I was so proud of her.

She was cautious though – typically – although other people didn't see that, she had such strong opinions on everything, from politics to babies, and she was forthright in expressing them. But me, I wasn't fooled. I was her mum, I'd known her all her life, I knew all about the inner self-doubt.

She'd been a stubborn kid, a bolshy teenager, all the more cussed because of her inner turmoil. I lost count of the number of times she stormed out of the house; the hours I spent scouring the kitchen, shampooing carpets, tidying cupboards, anything to stop myself imagining that this might be the time she wouldn't come back. I tried not to think what she might get up to once she went away to university, she was passionate about so many causes, but if she did flout the law I never heard of it.

But then Drew came into her life. He changed everything. Marriage, children, security, they brought out the best in her. Strange really, she'd always scoffed at my lack of ambition, but then she adopted so many of my ways.

She was right, of course. My horizons didn't rise above motherhood. Freddie, Kenyon, Elvira, Sally, they were the reason for my existence. That's why I lost the plot when Sally died ... and then when the other three left home.

Guy didn't need me. He was away most weeks anyway; he'd made a life without me. My fault again. All those trips abroad expanding his business empire, the dinners, the award ceremonies, the weekend retreats, I could have gone with him, but I preferred to stay at home, being there for the children.

Without them, who was I? The house was empty. I was empty.

The boys saw what was happening; they gave me the art classes for Christmas. Watercolours first, oils, acrylics, charcoal – I loved them all. I won two competitions, had a painting in a local exhibition, started to become a person in my own right. It was my money that turned our conservatory into a studio. Mine! The Open University followed – psychology, the humanities, history of art. Suddenly I had opinions.

Guy didn't notice. The washing and ironing happened, meals appeared as usual, he continued to use the house like a hotel. We co-existed quite amicably ... at least, I thought we did at the time.

Until he retired.

They gave him a terrific send-off, making him out to be a real paragon. Well, they always do, don't they, at retirement parties and funerals? But I honestly didn't recognise this man, Guy Beacham, they were lauding. 'Energetic', 'focused', 'driven'? Yes. But 'humorous'? 'compassionate'? 'sensitive'? Hello?

He gave that job everything, no question. But when you take everything away from everything there's nothing left; psychology taught me that. Now he had nowhere to go, nothing to do. This ... this stranger ... invaded my space, morning, noon and night, leaving coffee cups, newspapers, letters, books, lying everywhere. Changing things in the garden, accompanying me to the shops, to the library, on excursions with the grandchildren. Everything wound me up and I hardly ever painted. Even when I did manage to escape to my studio, he saw nothing amiss in coming in with coffee or chat. I tried explaining that any interruption was a disturbance too far when I was painting, but he just looked at me with that hurt expression, and I was left with guilt churning amongst the other furious emotions, the death knell to any creative expression, if ever there was one.

Freddie understood. 'Well, boot him out, Mother. Barricade yourself in. Send him on long errands.' But then, Freddie's artistic too. When things got worse he was blunt: 'Well, no point in hanging around if you feel that bad.'

Elvira, though, no, I couldn't talk to her about it. 'You chose him,' she said once when I was fed up about something he did. 'Talk to him. Tell him how you feel.' But you can't just talk; the other person has to listen. Guy had forgotten how to hear me – if he'd ever known.

Marriage for Elvira was something else. Drew idolised her, and the sparkle hadn't begun to diminish in the ten years they had together. Forty-one and a half years of marriage, though, that's a different story. Life changes people. I wasn't the shy, besotted girl I'd been at twenty-one; Guy wasn't the handsome, persuasive dynamo he'd been at twenty-five. And neither of us was ever the same after what happened to Sally. Since his retirement, being thrown together full time simply underlined our incompatibility.

That day, when the police came, I was thinking about Elvira, wondering how on earth I was going to tell her. It sounds sick, I know, but I might as well admit it: I actually envied her her widowhood. Talk about perverted! But what I saw was freedom. Of course, she'd had freedom forced upon her; she'd watched that vile disease rob Drew of everything, and she'd have given anything to keep him. How could I tell her that I was choosing to leave the man I married?

I must have been rehearsing what I'd say the very moment the accident happened. I'd lead into it, talk about symbolism, shading, perspective, and tell her about the shadows in her parents' lives. That's why I had to get that picture exactly right. Daft really, thinking about it now, as if it matters, but I cursed when the doorbell rang that day. I was so far away in my thoughts, I jumped, and the line between the end of the house and the sky smudged. 'Damn it!'

I heard Guy thudding down the stairs, clipping across the wooden floor in the hall, and I remember thinking, Well, at least he's a useful barrier between me and unwanted interruptions. So when I heard the footsteps coming closer, I was starting to feel that same old tension: Why can't he even do that *without bothering me? And that's when I heard him say, 'Carole, it's the police.'*

Even yet that whole experience runs in my mind like a slow motion film.

I lay down my palette. Then my brush. I wipe my fingers one by one on the rag I keep hung on the easel.

'Carole, there's been an accident.'

The smell of turps on my hand stifles the cry that never draws breath.

'PC Will Bartholomew,' the male officer says. He looks so young and nervous, clutching his hat. 'And this is Shirley Adams, our Family Liaison Officer.'

The woman's a bit older, comfortably rounded, calm.

She gives me a half smile, showing her crooked front teeth. I wonder if it's her job to train him in breaking bad news.

He stumbles on, the words sounding rehearsed. 'I'm afraid your daughter's been involved in a road traffic collision. She's at the Royal Infirmary now.'

I shake my head. 'Can't be. Not Elvira. Not my Ellie,' I say.

'I'm afraid so. She gave us your names as next of kin.'

Why didn't she phone us? I must get to her. But Guy holds me back. 'Sshh, wait a minute. Listen, Carole.'

The policewoman comes closer, steers me back to a chair, kneels beside me. 'I'm afraid she wasn't alone,' she says. 'She had her two little girls with her.'

And that's when I start shaking. No. No! NO!

'And?' Guy says. The world stops, waiting for that answer.

'I'm afraid they're both seriously injured too,' PC Bartholomew says. 'They've been taken to Sick Kids ... sorry, Sick Children's.'

All three of them ... All three of them!

'How bad is it?' Guy croaks.

'I'm sorry, it's not looking good. We think you should go to the hospital without delay.'

'Which one?' Guy sounds half his normal size.

'Whichever you think ...'

When no one answers the policewoman says tentatively, 'Maybe the Infirmary first? Check things out? Then we could take you ... one of you maybe, to Sick Children's?'

Next thing I know, we're in the back of a police car, blue lights flashing, scorching through the streets. Guy's holding my hand so hard it's crushing the rings against my fingers. And I'm thinking, What will the girls say when I tell them about the ride in a police car? What will Elvira say when I tell her I'm leaving her father?

Chapter 5

Oliver

OLIVER TOOK THE BACK road from Ellie's cottage, the vibrant greens and warm sun lifting his spirits, his mind barely registering the remote sound of a wailing siren. What a beautiful afternoon. No wonder Ellie had chosen this quiet backwater as her refuge, it was inspirational, even to a philistine like him.

He glanced at his watch. 3.50. Should be finished with his client in time to cook tea for the girls. He grimaced. If he was prepared to devote time to winning *Willow* round he must indeed be beyond redemption.

Willow: surely the most difficult child he'd ever encountered. She made no effort whatsoever to disguise her dislike of him; indeed it was her mission in life to speed his departure. But it was a case of love-me, love-my-child.

He hadn't been looking for romance. He'd been visiting a potential new client in the area when he saw the banners.

NEW COMMUNITY CENTRE OPENING
JOIN US FOR COFFEE AND SCONES

It was jam-packed with people; brimming with bonhomie.

'Grab a seat, anywhere you can find one.'

Ellie had patted the one beside her. 'Perch here. It's survival of the fittest today. Can't be choosy.'

He'd perched for ten minutes and been reeled into Ellie's life. The fact that one foot at the end of an extraordinarily long and shapely leg had been casually hooked around the bar of his stool had undoubtedly speeded the process.

It had been a shock realising he was preoccupied with thoughts – unseemly thoughts – about the wife of a dying man, but at least Ellie had no suspicions, he was quite sure about that. She was totally wrapped up in Drew's latest test results, Drew's weight loss, Drew's loss of appetite, Drew's next scan. At first her very innocence had added to the attraction. He could stare into her eyes while he listened to her latest worries; he could reach out and touch her arm on the pretext of comforting her; he could stay on after chauffeuring her from the hospital until it was only sensible to eat together, to sit close to her in the gathering gloom.

She hadn't known about Grace, his ex, at first. Or about the children, who waited in vain for their father to witness Barney coming first in the long-jump on sports day, to meet the teachers, to see Jane taking the principal part in the school end-of-year play. He told Ellie: 'Just you concentrate on you. We need to get you through this whole beastly business. I'm here to shore you up when the walls start crumbling. Lean on me. Who I am isn't important. I'm just your prop.'

Odd. He kept glancing at the clock. Surely Ellie said they'd be back for tea. She definitely did. *It'll take more than chicken and chips ...* her parting shot. Ah well, it wouldn't be the first time they'd had microwaved food because Ellie's timing didn't dovetail with his more rigid interpretation of six o'clock. Artistic licence she called it.

Strange really. He'd have been beyond annoyed if his ex had done that. The meal would be in the bin, her ears ringing with his rage. But somehow you couldn't do that with Ellie, she was too vulnerable, too near the edge.

What impulse had she followed tonight? Whose sob story was she listening to? And what kind of mood would Willow be in if she was hungry as well as irritable? Didn't bear thinking about. Maybe he should leave the food with a message and scarper. But then he wouldn't get the opportunity to ... No, he'd wait. Ellie'd probably just met up with some friend or other, lost track of time. The girls would be playing with the friend's kids, nibbling snacks, not wanting to leave either.

And she'd be so contrite when she got home. Not like Grace, militant in her absolute conviction that she was right. Always. Ellie was a mass of doubt and insecurity, she needed his reassurance. She needed him, full stop. He liked that.

He gave it another forty minutes, then rang her mobile. Switched off. Hell and damnation! Why did she *do* that? No point in carrying the blessed thing if she didn't even switch it on. He'd told her a million times, 'I want to be able to reach you. Tell you I love you.' She'd given him that enigmatic look, but she'd still left her phone off more often than on.

'You having an affair?' he'd asked her once.

'Yep,' she'd said, as if he'd caught her unawares.

He'd stared at her. 'You're not.' Buying time.

'Well, if you say so.'

'Ellie?'

'You asked me. I answered.'

'You're. Having. An. Affair?'

'You should know that better than anyone,' she'd flashed back.

'You mean ...?'

'With you, of course, dumb-head.'

'Riiight.'

'Well, am I not?'

'If you say so.'

'Meaning?' She'd stared at him with those penetrating hazel eyes.

'It's much more than that to me.' And he'd taken her in his arms and told her things he'd never said to any woman before. Tender things, committed things, things he might regret if Willow kept up her campaign of hostility.

But she hadn't reciprocated. She wouldn't make promises she might not be able to keep. And she couldn't be sure until Willow had melted.

Somebody calling himself PC Morgan was cagey.

'I'll just take down the particulars, sir. Check for you.'

'Would they know ... about accidents, or hospital admissions, or ... ?'

'They'd know about traffic, 999 calls for the police.'

'OK. And you'll let me know?'

'Are you a relative, sir?'

'Well, not exactly, but I'm her partner. I'm often here. Overnight.'

'Right, sir. But I take it you don't actually live at the same address?'

'Not all the time, no.'

'Just casual is it, then?'

'No, it bloody isn't,' Oliver exploded, muttering under his breath. 'If that's any of your damn business.' Tread on my most sensitive corns, why don't you?

'Only checking the facts, sir. No offence intended.' But plenty given! 'So how long have you and she been an item, as they say?'

Damnably hard to know. What did it depend on? Ellie knowing how he felt? Ellie returning his affection? Ellie agreeing at last to sleep with him?

'About five months.' Long enough for him to be sure, for it to be anything but casual.

'Ahh. And you say you expected Ms Kennedy home by ... when?'

'By six.'

'Right. I'll check that out for you then, sir.'

Chapter 6

Lennox

THE WHOLE STATION seemed to be buzzing with the news.

The young PCs had decked out the coffee room with a banner: CONGRATULATIONS, sparkling in silver with miniscule pink, white and blue bootees hung from each letter. Everyone had signed a card: more congratulations, as if *he'd* done something heroic. His PA had filled a vase – with pink roses, for goodness' sake! – put it bang in the middle of his desk, just to make sure he noticed probably. At lunchtime she'd tentatively handed him a parcel wrapped in the palest pink tissue paper, tied up with curls of white ribbon, with a cautious 'Just a wee something for the little one', as if she was afraid he'd ask to see the receipt, mutter things about accountability for taxpayers' money. And everywhere he went the air echoed with good wishes. 'Brilliant news, boss.' 'Give Toni our best.' 'Got a name yet, guv?' 'Got any photos?' 'Hope you're coming to the Three Nuns tonight, sir. Wet the baby's head.' Everybody would be there, they said.

Lennox was touched. Not that he'd let them see it. Nobody respected a mushy boss, not in his business.

But he couldn't settle. He kept seeing that tiny wrinkled face, nestling in the crook of his elbow, feeling the soft lift and fall of that fragile breath. Nicole Maggie. Nicole Maggie. It would trip off the tongue eventually. Maggie after her grandmother – it gave Lennox a thrill knowing that. Because he still loved Margaret Claire McKenzie to pieces, even after nearly thirty years.

She was twenty-eight, with strawberry-blonde curls and navy blue eyes, when she'd been directed to him, a new lecturer at the university with her first big research grant.

'Basically I want to find out what happens to kids who commit crimes before the age of responsibility,' she'd explained.

He hadn't a clue, but he'd sure as hell find out. He'd pestered every senior detective and every protection officer he could lay hands on. He'd searched the records for the high profile cases that made the headlines. He'd rummaged through police files for the more obscure examples, giving Maggie insights – stripped of identifying detail, of course; he was scrupulous about that. And the more he dug, the more he'd been sucked into her project. He'd never before realised how many kids did terrible inexplicable things, he'd never before felt their families' anguish, and he'd never before felt so alive.

He held his breath when she got her PhD and was offered a job in London. She took it, of course she did; too good a chance to throw away. But he wasn't about to lose the best thing that had ever happened to him. It became his constant mission to make darn sure she didn't forget him. 'Got a permanent seat reservation on the 6pm train every Friday. Her or me,' he boasted.

Two years after she became Dr McKenzie and started travelling the conference circuit, she took on the mantle of Mrs Lennox McRobert in her private life. He watched his Maggie sleeping some mornings before he left for work and wondered all over again what kept her chained to an emotionally retarded policeman who needed a PA to sort out his sentence structure.

And his heart swelled with pride to see her, two generations later, wrapping Nicole Maggie up in her all-encompassing love.

Everyone told him being a grandparent was all the fun, all the joy, without the responsibility, but when they laid that new life in his arms he felt overwhelmed by the weight of his role. How could you protect such innocence from the blackness of the world she'd newly slithered into? It was his *job*, he was *trained* to deal with tragedy, clean up society, but every single day he drew breath reminded him that even he was only scratching the surface. Nicole Maggie, his own precious granddaughter, was going to walk alone one day all too soon in a world full of fast cars, thieves, rapists, murderers. He wanted to smuggle her away to a parallel universe where nothing sordid or cruel could ever touch her.

The phone startled him out of his reverie.

'Inspector Lennox McRobert speaking.'

People with causes ... departmental budgets ... crime statistics ... court summons ... reports of incidents ... demands for action ... Nicole Maggie was soon relegated by the sheer welter of work. But it was a struggle to concentrate today. Must be the euphoria of yesterday. Or was it the fear of tomorrow?

Chapter 7

Lennox

IT WAS THE INSPECTOR'S choice to attend the scene of the crash. His officers were perfectly capable, but he really needed to get out. A breath of honest-to-goodness real life might shake off this ridiculous distraction and put him back into police mode.

The articulated lorry lay like a monstrous orange beetle marooned on its side, its head resting in the bushes, its swollen abdomen jack-knifed across the whole road. Dwarfed by its antagonist, what was left of a red Fiat screamed to be noticed, its brilliant colour undimmed even in its death throes. Brown and green ants with phosphorescent markings wove a scavenging dance around and over and into the carnage.

Lennox nodded to the sergeant and moved in closer. A man, white Caucasian, early fifties, five-ten or so, sandy hair, clean-shaven face the colour of death, sat on the bank, head between his legs. All four limbs intact, no visible blood, no obvious injury. Crouched beside him, Sergeant Naismith would be doing her best not to inhale the sour smell of vomit (no alcohol you could detect) as she offered rule-book comfort, waiting for him to unglue his paralysed tongue. Poor sod, whatever the rights and wrongs, this moment would be branded on his brain for the rest of his life. And no chance of him getting straight back into his lorry and driving off before he lost his bottle. Not with this mess.

'What've we got?'

'Woman, mid-thirties, two little girls, guv, roughly eight-nine-ish and three-ish, I'd guess. Not looking good. Mother's trapped by her legs, conscious at first, not now. Older kid's not responding but still got a heartbeat. Little one – looks like she's gone.'

'Any names?'

'Driver's an Elvira Kennedy. Says the kids are Willow and Madeline.'

'Next-of-kin?'

'Her parents.'

'Anybody contacted them?'

'Bartholomew and Adams are just waiting for information about which hospital, then they're on their way, sir.'

The scream of sirens cut through the catalogue as a second fire-engine raced along the road towards them. The men were out of the truck before the wheels stopped turning, and Lennox heard their suppressed curses as they peered into the Fiat. It was always the same where children were involved. But there was no time wasted in idle emotion. A muttered exchange, a few curt orders, and the scene lit up like a macabre witches' firework display: angle grinders slicing off the roof of the car, stray beams glinting on plastic, metal, fluids, as the paramedics plied their mysterious trade.

Once the vehicle was bisected Lennox moved in closer. The woman's legs were pumping blood, her once-white tee shirt was stained a deep crimson, her face completely drained of colour, no sign of any consciousness now, no cries of pain, no wailing of her daughters' names. Her long red hair swung over the blue Lycra legs of the older girl as the men lifted the child out to begin the mammoth task of keeping her alive ... Lycra legs ... half a minute ...

'Excuse *me*!' the paramedic snapped.

'Sorry. Sorry.' Lennox moved hastily to one side.

A fireman stepped back from the hole in the front of the Fiat with the passenger seat in his hands as if it were no more solid than a portable booster for a toddler ... the kind of thing Lennox had been looking at in the catalogues, mentally registering he'd need one for Nicole Maggie before long. He gritted his teeth. Focus, man, focus. This isn't the time. He peered closer ... took another step forward.

Something blue lay in the jagged space. Lennox felt nausea flood his mouth. 'Jeez.'

A fireman leaned into the car and instantly backed out yelling, 'Kelly! Get some ice over here. And a sterile bag. *Yesterday*!'

Somebody ran towards the ambulance, back to the wreck. The man who'd shouted leaned into the space, picked something up, lifted it over and out, slid it into the opened bag. The runner took off as if he'd been handed an Olympic relay baton. A motorbike engine revved. It was gone.

A black ballet shoe lay upside down on the road a metre away from the Fiat.

Lennox watched mesmerised as two paramedics rolled the girl onto a stretcher, wrapped more compression bandages over the bloodied stump of her right thigh, covered her in another foil blanket and lifted her into the ambulance. Slamming the door on the three choreographed figures, a colleague slapped the side of the vehicle and it shot off, screaming its urgency in diminishing echoes. The man turned and Lennox saw his face, grey, crumpled. He shook his head, his lips set in a grim line.

An ominous silence remained. The scene unravelled in slow motion. More sparks as the angle grinder attacked the offside door. A paramedic vanished inside. The world held its breath. An eternity later he was backing out of the space where once the girl with the flaming hair had closed the door to keep her baby safe, in his arms a bundle of pink. Nicole Maggie in a couple of years' time. He laid her gently on the ground and three more figures crowded in, blocking the totally inert figure from Lennox's view. But he'd seen it all before: the rhythm of resuscitation. By the time he could see the child again she was wired up to machines and drips and strapped onto a stretcher, a tiny mound surrounded by gentle giants.

'OK, chaps. Let's get this show on the road,' somebody shouted.

They handled the child like precious porcelain.

Lennox waited long enough to get the lorry driver's stuttering outline. She'd 'shot roon the corner like a bat ooto hell', he 'niver stood a chance', he 'hadnae a drap o' anyfin since last Saturday'. Then with a nod at the policemen measuring, calculating, shaking their heads, the inspector walked back to his car. The ballet shoe lay where it had fallen.

'Bring it to me when the CI's finished,' he muttered to his sergeant, jerking his head in the direction of the shoe. 'I'll see it gets to the family.'

He'd better get back to the office, all those reports, all the statistics waiting for him, his PA, mystified but loyal, stalling for him ...

Even so, he turned left at the crossroads instead of right. He couldn't stop himself. He simply had to check that Nicole Maggie was all in one piece. Still breathing.

Toni was startled by his appearance, he could see that, even before the tentative, 'Dad?' Not that he told her about the kiddie in blue Lycra, or the toddler in pink, or the black ballet shoe that was full of warm foot one minute and then lying empty on the road the next.

He stood staring down at the sleeping baby – 'Please don't wake her, Dad. I've only just got her off to sleep' – wondering all over again how he was ever going to bear the burden of responsibility.

Will Bartholomew was back at the station by the time Lennox returned to his desk.

'How'd it go?' Lennox said.

'Mother was hysterical, guv. Says the son-in-law died coupla years ago. Cancer. Doesn't know how the daughter'll cope if anything happens to the kids.'

'And has it?'

'Not last I heard. But they don't hold out much hope – for either of them.'

Lennox shook his head not daring to speak.

'Mr Beacham, the father, he's holding it together, but he couldn't leave his wife in that state, so we drove them both up to the Infirmary. She'd got a bit more of a grip by the time we got there.'

'Sobering places, hospitals.'

'Aye.' A pause. Then an echoing, 'Aye.'

'OK. You get off home, Bartholomew. Enough's enough. Tell the duty officer to keep me posted.'

'Thank you, guv. Night.'

He was deep in a report from HQ when PC Callum Morgan rapped on the door.

'Bartholomew told me you wanted to be kept in the picture about that RTC, sir. There's a guy on the phone says he's Elvira Kennedy's sort-of partner, and he wants to know if there's any reports of an accident or anything, because she isn't home and she should be. Only, the thing is, sir, the parents said there wasn't a bloke on the scene now, and they're her next-of-kin. They said Mrs Kennedy lived alone with the two girls since the husband died.'

'Any more news on the kids?'

'The FLO, Adams, rang through about ten minutes ago. Seems the wee one's not responding to anything. Other one's still hanging in there. '

'OK. Put him through,' barked Lennox. 'What's his name?'

'Oliver Reynolds.'

'Right. Thanks. I'll take it from here.'

'Sir.'

Lennox pulled the phone towards him, picked up a pen, wrote on the notepad in front of him.

'Hello? Hello?'

'Hello. Mr Reynolds?'

'Yes, who am I speaking to *now*?'

'Inspector Lennox McRobert.' He emphasised his title. A bit of clout wouldn't go amiss. 'I understand you're enquiring about the whereabouts of Elvira Kennedy.'

'Yes. I told the other officers.'

'Would you mind telling *me*, sir?'

'She left a few minutes before half three to take the kids to ballet, but she hasn't come back. They eat at six. I can't reach her on her mobile and the dance teacher's gone home and I don't know who else might know where she's gone. So I just thought I'd check if there's been an accident or anything, if her car's broken down.'

'And you are?'

'I'm her ... well, sort of partner. Only I don't actually live here all the time. I come and go. You know what it's like. The kids have to get used to me.'

'Are you at Mrs Kennedy's address at the moment, Mr Reynolds?'

'Yeees. Why?'

'Could you stay there, please. I'll come over.'

'But ...'

'Give me, let's say thirty minutes.'

He hung up before the man could winkle anything more out of him. Well, you couldn't be too careful. The press would stoop to anything to get a good story.

Oliver Reynolds didn't match his voice. He was bigger (six feet four-ish) and older (forty-ish), darker (shock of black curls, olive skin) and less assertive (twisting hands, darting glances). And the gold cufflinks, expensive suit, polished shoes, didn't fit with the muddled state of the house, the shabbiness, the assorted girls' trainers and Wellingtons discarded in the hallway, toys and books scattered about the living room, unwashed dishes in what Lennox could see of the kitchen.

But it all made sense. The table was set for four, the smell of chips hanging in the air. And there was no mistaking the flame-haired woman beside Reynolds in the photo he carried in his wallet.

'I'm afraid I have bad news, Mr Reynolds.'

All credit to him, the bloke didn't go to pieces. Asked questions, listened to the answers, lost his colour, clenched his teeth, but he held on. Lennox was grateful. Grown men crying was what he couldn't take. It reminded him of ... No, don't even go there.

'I'm happy to give you a lift to the Infirmary.'

'Thanks, but I'll take my car. Then I'll have it to get back after ...'

'Pricey business parking out there these days,' Lennox

dropped in conversationally.

'Even so, best to have my own wheels.'

'Fair enough. Sorry to be the bearer of such bad news.'

Lennox watched him gather up his jacket and keys, climb into his car and roar off down the road. If he'd been out on patrol himself he'd have flagged the guy down, but he hoped devoutly that none of his men was on the alert near the Royal Infirmary tonight. Oliver Reynolds deserved a break right now.

Chapter 8

The medical team

THE SURGEON STRETCHED his aching muscles. Eight hours bending over the operating table took its toll these days. He took a bite of a chocolate biscuit, washed it down with extra-strong black tea, and resumed writing up his notes.

The final summary brought home the extent of Elvira Kennedy's injuries: subdural haematoma, fractured pelvis, ribs and sternum, ruptured spleen and uterus, pneumothorax, compound fractures of both legs, just for starters. Between them they'd stemmed the blood loss, relieved the pressure in her head, dealt with the most urgent life-threatening problems, but she'd have her work cut out recovering from this little lot. If she survived at all.

Why didn't she tell us about Oliver?

We'd just come back from seeing Maddie. Maddie! ... my baby ... broken beyond repair. Outwardly unmarked, her beautiful little self. Inside ... her spinal cord severed on impact, right near the top. C3/4, they said, whatever that means. And her brain's swelling up. There's no room inside her skull, so it's cutting off the blood supply to ... I can't bear to think about it. My baby. My Maddie.

There's nothing anybody can do now, they said. Not even her Granny who'd give her life if it would help. I couldn't bear watching the machine filling her up with pretend breaths; feeling her little fingers, limp, not returning my clasp; hearing words that mean she won't ever again run towards me with that huge grin of delight on her face; ever again fling her arms around my neck; ever again send me a card smothered in hugs and kisses. Ever, ever again.

I had to get back to Elvira. She mustn't give up. Willow needs her. We need her.

'Best not say anything about Madeline to her mum at the moment,' they said. I don't think I'll ever be able to say anything to anybody, full stop, not with that picture of Maddie filling the space.

And there he was, a stranger, *standing over my Ellie, touching her hair, her face, her hand, even the bruise below her ear. He looked up when we walked in. There were tears on his cheeks.*

'You must be her parents,' he said. 'I'm Oliver.' As if that told us everything.

'Oliver?' Guy said.

He ignored the question, half whispering behind his hand, 'How are they? The girls?'

Guy shook his head, one finger on his lips. He mouthed 'Maddie' and cut the air with his hand.

Oliver closed his eyes and gritted his teeth.

He looked down at Elvira, touched her cheek softly, and then walked over to us. 'She'd want to donate Maddie's organs,' he murmured out of the side of his mouth.

I felt as if my whole body was screaming. They said, don't tell her ...

'Hold on a min ...' Guy started to say, but this Oliver person interrupted.

'We talked about it and she put her name on the register. It's what she would want. And there isn't time to hang around.'

How did he know? She never talked to me about it, and I've known her all her life. It was too much, a stranger *telling us what to do with our precious granddaughter, our Maddie, who wasn't even properly dead yet.*

'I think you should leave,' I said, my teeth clenched.

But he didn't.

'Imagine if it was Maddie needing an organ,' he

persisted. 'What would you say then?'

I tried to shush him: 'Not in front of ...', but he ignored me.

'We'd want some other family to be brave and unselfish, wouldn't we?'

'We?' I squealed. 'We? This is nothing to do with you. This is our daughter. Our granddaughter.'

I couldn't bear it. I rushed out of the room and locked myself in the toilet, sobbing.

I don't know how long it was before I heard Guy outside, the darkness made it hard to see my watch. In any case time had ceased to mean anything.

'Carole? The doctors want to talk to us. Are you coming?'

I had to be there.

'And before you lose it again, I've said Oliver can come too. Ellie would want him to know.'

The relatives' room seemed suffocating already when the two doctors walked in.

'My name's Josh Goddard. I'm the ICU consultant. As I think you know, Elvira took the full force of the impact on the right side of her chest, her abdomen and legs. She has multiple fractures and crush injuries. We've managed to stop the bleeding, and it's now a matter of waiting to see how successful that's been. We can't say at this stage how things will develop abdominally, or with the legs. The next forty-eight hours will be critical.'

'The legs?' The boyfriend's voice cracked.

The mother covered her mouth with her hands.

'They're badly crushed. It's impossible to know if we can save them at the moment. There's extensive damage. She's not strong enough for us to do anything more than immobilise them at the moment.'

'You might not ... save them?' It came out as a hoarse whisper.

'The injuries are very severe. We can't rule it out, but let's just wait and see. The head injury is our biggest concern right now.'

The boyfriend was ashen. Small wonder. Yesterday Elvira had been a beautiful woman. Head injured, sawn off at the thighs, horribly scarred, it'd be a whole different picture.

'We're monitoring her closely and we'll keep you informed, but I must stress again, she's critically ill. *Critically*. She's sustained massive injuries. We can't promise you anything. I think you should prepare yourselves for the worst.'

Carole Beacham looked as if she might faint, but at least she'd stopped that infernal wailing. Guy Beacham sat staring as if his mind was completely elsewhere.

But there was more. 'This is Mr Bannerjee, one of our senior neurosurgeons. I'll hand over to him to tell you about a particularly serious complication.'

All eyes swivelled to the Indian, his green scrubs creased and stained with damp patches, a mask still hanging round his neck. He presented an odd picture, his totally white hair at odds with his young face.

'As Dr Goddard says, your daughter has sustained major impact injuries in the crash,' he said, every word clear, only a hint of his eastern inheritance slipping through in his intonation. 'One of the most serious is to her brain, caused by the head being slammed backwards and forwards, and by a penetrating wound. Apparently she was conscious when the paramedics arrived at the scene, but lost consciousness soon after. We scanned her head and the pictures showed a splinter of metal lodged in her brain. And a clot – rather a large clot, I'm afraid. What we call a subdural haematoma. We've removed the metal and the blood, but we can't tell at this stage what impact this will have had on her functioning. We can't rule out serious brain damage.'

'But they said … she was talking … she said …' You could hear the mother's tongue sticking in her parched mouth.

'Indeed. It seems she was able to respond to direct questions initially – her name, the names of the girls, next of kin – before she lost consciousness.'

'Doesn't that mean … her brain was … working normally?' The relatives always grasped at straws, it was only natural, needing something to cling to while they drowned.

'It's impossible to draw any firm conclusions at this stage. The brain as you know is made up of different parts, each controlling different functions, and the metal we removed had embedded itself quite deeply, transversely. Even though we know from the X-rays we've removed all of it, we can't tell at this stage what damage the splinter did in cutting through the tissue. Only time will tell.'

Mr Goddard nodded his agreement and resumed the explanation. 'What happens after an injury like this is that the brain swells up – just as your finger will swell up if you give it a bang. But the skull is a hard unyielding box; there's limited space inside, so if the brain expands, it forces itself down through the hole where the spinal cord joins the brain.'

He sketched the anatomy, circling the vital junction on a blank sheet of paper.

'Elvira's brain has swollen up a lot, and because of the increase in size, it's in danger of pressing down on the brain stem and cutting off the blood supply there, which, as you'll appreciate, is a serious worry. So we've cut a small window out of her skull to give the brain some more space, and put in a little instrument to monitor the pressure, and we're giving her medication to help reduce the swelling: Manitol, which is a kind of diuretic, and steroids. And as you've seen, we've got her propped up with her head quite high to help with drainage too.'

'How soon will it be before you can let her wake up?' The boyfriend again.

'We can't say anything for sure at this stage,' Dr Goddard said gently. 'Our plan at the moment is to keep her fully sedated in Intensive Care and watch her progress. If she seems to be responding to the treatment we're giving her, we might try to lighten the level of consciousness and see how she goes. But again, as Mr Bannerjee says, we have to warn you that the situation is very grave indeed. Elvira has sustained multiple injuries – extremely serious injuries, and the next few hours will be critical. You should feel free to visit any time, stay for as long as you wish. And please, don't hesitate to ask if you need any more information. Inasfar as we're able to give it, we'll keep you fully in the picture.'

Everyone knew that was bad – visit any time, stay for as long as you like. Might as well come right out with it: say goodbye while you can.

Three hours and twenty minutes later the consultant surgeon was summonsed back to Elvira's bedside. Her pulse was racing, blood pressure in her boots. They'd have to go in again, find the bleeder. The thought crossed his mind: she might be better served by inaction. Who would want to go on, knowing they'd killed both their children? Well, OK, technically the older one wasn't dead yet, but it was probably only a matter of time.

Chapter 9

Oliver

AT LEAST SITTING beside her, Oliver knew Ellie was still fighting for her life.

For once he had her all to himself. Her parents had gone to see their granddaughters. They were in a daze, torn in three directions. Which one needed them most?

There was no conflict of interest for him though; visiting Willow would be enough to put her back days. But with nothing to do except hold Ellie's inert hand, the thoughts he didn't want to consider escaped from his control.

His eyes took in the immobile form, swathed in a white sheet, a cradle holding even that weight off her crushed legs. His mind raced ahead. What would it be like making love … if she was only a … trunk? Those beautiful legs he'd admired, caressed, gripped … that she'd curled around him … gone … cut off … abandoned … What if there was no recognition in her eyes …

He couldn't go there. He *mustn't*. Not yet at least.

Was it his fault? If he hadn't been staying at the cottage …

What if he'd taken his own children to Tenerife that week as Grace had wanted, instead of telling her he absolutely couldn't get away from work? He saw little enough of Barney and Jane as it was … But Grace had always been manipulative, she'd have chained him so close to her schedules that there'd have been no room at all for Ellie.

What if he'd insisted on replacing the Fiat with a four-wheel-drive as he'd wanted Ellie to do ever since she'd told him about skidding on the ice in January, ending up facing the wrong way in the opposite ditch? It was only great good fortune there was nothing else on the road at that moment on that day.

What if he'd left her in peace yesterday, given her space to be ready in good time for Willow's exhibition dance, to leave on time, not have to rush? If he'd not detained her for that extra kiss? Allowing her to slow to twenty-five miles an hour on that narrow stretch just before the bend, instead of the thirty-eight or -nine they reckoned she must have been travelling.

What if he'd simply said, 'Let Maddie stay with me. You concentrate on Willow,' avoiding the tantrums, the tension, the pressure?

What if he'd made more effort to get Willow onside, then he could have been driving her to the dance class himself instead of Ellie that day? She'd still be safe and whole and at home with Maddie right now.

If only ...

He leaned closer.

'Oh, Ellie, forgive me. I've been a selfish beast. I wanted you all to myself. You're the best thing that ever happened to me. I love your generosity, your kindness, your sparkle, your sense of fun, your beautiful body ... everything about you. And I don't mind the instant meals, honestly. I was only winding you up. Please, please don't give up.

'I want to take you to Florence ... remember? And Norway. Remember that hotel we looked at in the brochure, made of ice, reindeer skins on the beds? And that painted canal boat we saw the other day, where we could be totally alone together? So many places I want to take you.

'I want to make every day wonderful. Make a proper home with you, be a dad to your girls – a much better dad than I've been to Barney and Jane. Marry me, Ellie. I promise you, I'll grow to love Willow. I love you sooo much, I'll be there for you, whatever happens. Just come back to me. Please, please, *please*.'

Chapter 10

Oliver

ELVIRA'S TWO BROTHERS appeared before her parents returned. Hard to believe these two nondescript men were related to her. Grey, exhausted from their breakneck journeys from Chester and Durham, they seemed to shrink further inside themselves at the sight of their sister, pain etching deeper grooves into their drawn faces.

Oliver shook hands, stooped to kiss Ellie, and backed outside. He didn't wait to see the reunion with their parents; he couldn't take any more of the mother's wailing.

He got as far as sitting in the car, switching on the engine, but then found he simply couldn't drive away. He tried dozing with the seat tilted back, but it was hopeless. How could he seek oblivion when Ellie's life might be ticking towards its end?

The Beachams didn't seem surprised when he wandered into ICU at 2am, but no one moved, no one relinquished a hand for him. He had to settle for a seat in the corner listening to the sough and click of the machines rhythmically forcing each breath into her lungs.

He must have been hovering somewhere in a twilight zone when the alarms sounded. Five blue-clad figures leapt into action. Somehow he and Ellie's family were manoeuvred out of the room. He managed a quick glance towards the bed before the door closed behind them; a halo of red hair ... hands everywhere ... a syringe ...

It was eerily quiet in the relatives' room, a safe distance

away from the action, but every fibre of his being longed to be back with her, knowing second by second how the battle was going. No one spoke. No one dared.

When the door finally opened they knew.

The ICU consultant came straight to the point. 'I'm so sorry. We did everything we could. I'm afraid Elvira died a few minutes ago.'

'No! No! No!' Carole screamed. 'No! You have to go back! You must! You have to do something. You *must* save her!'

Oliver wanted to slap her, but the doctor seemed unfazed by her outburst. 'I'm so, so sorry. It's simply not possible. Her injuries were too severe. There was nothing more we could do.'

Both her sons held her, rocking her, everybody weeping.

Oliver slunk out of the room. He couldn't bear hysterics, especially not right now.

The nurses both looked up as he entered.

'Can I ... see her?'

'Of course. We're just tidying her up, but please, come this side. We'll be done in a minute.'

Standing staring down at Ellie, still faintly pink, her chest still rising and falling, her hand still warm, Oliver hesitated. He glanced up at the nurse now standing on the opposite side of the bed. 'They said ... has she ... really ... gone?'

'I'm afraid she has, yes.'

'But she's ...'

'We're keeping her body oxygenated until the specialist nurses have had a chance to talk to her parents about the organs. That side of things is nothing to do with us, but it's important to keep everything functioning normally, in case.'

'It's what she wanted. She told me. We talked about it.'

'That's good to know, but we have to be sensitive to the family's wishes too. The organ donation people are trained in this kind of thing. But knowing Elvira herself wanted it could be a useful way in. Thanks.'

Oliver reached for Ellie's hand. He stooped to kiss her cheek. It felt warm and soft to his lips.

'Don't go, Ellie,' he whispered. 'Please don't go. I love you. I need you. Please don't go.'

He was unaware of the tears falling until someone slipped a tissue into his free hand.

He wasn't there when Carole Beacham saw her daughter for the first time after death was pronounced, but he heard the unearthly keening. And this time he understood. It was eerie. Ellie didn't look dead, she didn't feel dead, she didn't sound dead. Surely there must be some mistake. No wonder Carole was adamant: taking Elvira's organs would be tantamount to murder.

But he *was* there when Sarah Jenkins, the specialist nurse in organ donation, talked to the family. Knowing he had to keep his mouth firmly shut this time, Oliver had space to observe the interplay between the various players. And watching Sarah was hypnotic. She couldn't be even as old as he was, yet she had an air of authority that was undeniable. She was professionally neat rather than elegant, a pretty-enough brunette rather than the sort of flamboyantly lovely girl you'd turn to look at a second time, yet you felt she was exactly the kind of person you'd want beside you in a crisis.

Somehow she managed to creep between the sobs and plant her arguments in the little furrows behind Carole's words. She seemed to understand exactly the doubts and fears, even empathise with the distress and pain, and yet retrieve a glimmer of hope out of carnage.

The '*senseless waste*' ... need not be totally meaningless ... a chance to help some other grieving family ... more than one, if you agree.

Feeling '*so helpless*' ... there is actually something you could do ... help you not to feel so powerless, prevent some other family from feeling as you do now.

'*Hardest of all for a mother*' ... you could reach out to another mother who loves her child devotedly too, who's at this very moment watching them slipping away.

'*Why didn't she tell us she carried a card?*' ... probably didn't want to trouble you with thoughts of her death ... shows the kind of daughter you raised ... special kind of bravery ... give her death a new meaning ... something you can do for her.

'*It would feel like killing her*' ... she really is dead already ... if we were to switch off the machines everything would stop ... if you give her organs, parts of her will live on ... giving life to others.

'*Did it make a difference, her carrying a donor card? Would they have tried harder if she hadn't?*' ... nobody could have done more ... several teams of surgeons all fighting for her ... highest priority patient in the whole hospital ... did everything humanly possible ... no expense, no effort spared ... doctors will show you evidence of the damage if you could bear it ... nobody would put retrieving organs above saving Elvira's own life ... besides the clinical team who cared for her have nothing to do with decisions about organ donation. The transplant team only come into play once there's nothing more that can be done for her.

Oliver couldn't help but be impressed.

But still Carole hesitated.

And then Willow took a turn for the worse, and Guy surprised everyone by saying to his hysterical wife, 'If a transplant would save her, would you want one?'

'Of course I would!' she snapped.

'Just like those other grandparents, other mothers, out there watching their precious children and grandchildren dying in front of their eyes,' Guy said, before turning and walking away.

In the canteen Oliver saw Sarah again, but she wasn't alone. Two men sat at the same table, a guy in a dog-collar and an older medic in blue scrubs. They were deep in conversation so he didn't like to interrupt.

Chapter 11

Carole

THIS CAN'T BE HAPPENING. I want to wake up and find this was all a nightmare.

I want to go back to being a perfectly ordinary family, with our ups and downs, but nothing dramatic.

I don't want to be torn in two like this. I don't want to make decisions, dread the consequences.

A tenth of my brain knows that Ellie doesn't need me now. Nor does Maddie. But everything in me shrieks, Don't waste a second of the precious time you have left before they go beyond your reach. Remember Sally ...

Yet I have *to leave them. Willow needs me, now more than ever. She needs me to talk to her. I must save her at least. The nurses say that on some level she may be aware that I'm here. I've read about this kind of thing: relatives, friends, talking, talking, talking, bringing their loved one back from the brink of whatever's next. And now there's only me to do that.*

'*Remember when Daddy took you to the zoo and you hid in the reptile house and drove him half out of his mind before you were found?*

'*And that time you chopped off the front of your hair and stuffed it in the guinea pig's cage so he could line a nest for himself. What a fright you looked! Mummy took you to the hairdresser to get the whole lot shortened, but even the professionals couldn't do much with it. You'd hacked it almost to your scalp. Of course it grew in time. And look at your hair now. Gorgeous. The nurses let me brush it. It's something I can do.*

'And remember when you found your advent calendar in November? You took all the chocolates out, and filled the wrappers with lumps of play-doh. Why you weren't sick eating that lot in a oner, I don't know. Good job Mummy found out before Maddie ate any, eh?

'What a rascal you were, young lady. You're so like your Mummy when she was your age. But we love you all the same, and we're going to have such fun, you and me, once you're out of here.

'I'm going to make a list of places we'll visit, things we'll do together. Remember, you wanted to make cinder toffee? Well, as soon as you're well enough, we'll have a go at that. You'll need to be extra careful though, sit right up to the table. Sugar mixture gets terribly hot. Can't have you scalding yourself now, can we?'

The picture of Willow in a wheelchair threatens to overwhelm me. I rush on.

'There's a card here from your wee friend, Jessie. Hand delivered. Remember Jessie? Your dancing pal? Shall I read it to you? You'll understand it better than I do.

'She says:

Hi Willow

I hope your *(oh, look, she can't spell you're)* feeling better.

I'm really fed up. My ballet teacher reckons I'm not ready for en pointe work after all. I know I am though. I mean, how can she say my ankles aren't strong enough? I've been practising, practising, practising like crazy at home. Just like you said, remember?

I can't wait to see you. Your my bestest friend in the whole world. Only they say I can't come yet. Mean, isn't it?

And guess what? You've really really got to be better by September 14. Our dance school is putting on a show. And it's not one of the ones everybody knows. It's been written speshially for us. How cool is that? I play a street urchin. That sounds gross, I know, but acktually the costumes are fab, and mine's all swirly and dark and mysteryus. You'll love it.

Get well soon. You absolutely can't miss this show.

With love from
Jessie

PS. I miss you.

'There, Willow, that'll be great, won't it? Seeing Jessie dancing as a street urchin. You know her better than I do, of course, but I rather suspect she'd prefer to be a princess, in a frilly snow-white tutu, than an urchin. Am I right? But we'll see. You hurry and get better and I promise I'll take you to see her.

'And here's another card. Wow, it's a big one. From all your classmates in P5. And the teacher, Mrs Swain. Remember? Funny to think they're all hard at work at school right now, isn't it? Some of them have drawn wee pictures for you. So sweet.

'Hurry up and open your eyes and you can see all your cards and flowers and books and toys and balloons.

'Grandpa's coming this afternoon. He's going to read you some Skulduggery Pleasant. You love those stories, don't you, honey? And I'll be back later. Promise. Wouldn't it be great if you were awake when I come back? Try, darling, try really hard. We want to see you smile, hear your voice, play games again.

'I'll bring in Monarchs of Scotland, shall I? And Pictionary. And Scrabble. And Cluedo. You can go first, and *you can be red. And it'd be much more fun than lying there sleeping all the time, don't you think?*

'You always love playing games, remember? Before I can clear one away you're asking, "What shall we do next, Granny?" Open your eyes and I promise I'll play games all day long. And you won't have to help tidy up. Just wake up, Willow. Please, please. Time to wake up.

'Is this light hurting your eyes, sweetie? The nurses need to see you're OK, but we could dim it a bit between times if it's giving you a headache. Ahh, here come the nurses.'

How can they be so relentlessly cheery, seeing what they see, doing what they do?

'Hi, Willow. We're back. Just going to give you a wee freshen up. Granny can come back in once we're done.'

'See you soon, darling. Love you loads and loads and loads.'

Chapter 12

Sarah

SARAH LEANED BACK in her chair and massaged her neck. She had the papers already assembled, just waiting for Carole and Guy Beacham to give the nod – well, Carole, really; she seemed to be the one with her foot on the brake.

Negotiations were always sensitive, often taxing, but they didn't get much tougher than this. First the death of a young son-in-law, then the accident. An unknown boyfriend appearing. Losing a granddaughter, then a daughter. Grim didn't describe it.

No wonder they were procrastinating. Car crashes, death, transplants, they happened to 'other people'. Seeing loved ones damaged beyond repair was shock enough, without vultures hovering wanting their organs.

Even so, she felt the familiar surge of impatience. It was a race against time to get everyone and everything into position ready for multiple exchanges – families, organs, histories, assessments, scan results, blood tests, authorisation forms, surgical teams, transport vehicles ... But you couldn't rush things. Not until the donor family were ready. You couldn't force the pace of that last goodbye. You couldn't raise hopes prematurely; you couldn't waste resources with surgeons standing about kicking their heels. But if you prepared carefully, before the ink was dry on the signatures you could instantly galvanise every player into action to maximise the chance of life for a lot of people. And this was where she excelled.

'You'd schedule your grandmother's demise if you could,' her father had laughed, back in the days when she'd lived at home and organised the family's timetabling.

'Driven' was one boyfriend's word for it.

That innate compulsion to create order out of chaos stood her in good stead now in her professional life, that, and her empathy. Somehow she knew what it felt like from the inside. And what she couldn't imagine, people confided.

So why couldn't she get insight into the Beachams' torment? The non-verbals screamed tension, terror even, but no one was unravelling the confusion for her.

Thank goodness for the chaplain. She was used to him popping up everywhere in the hospital, always sympathetic, always reassuring. Lately she'd wondered ... she pushed the thought out of reach. He was only doing his job.

Tea and doughnuts in the canteen was his suggestion.

'Better skip the doughnut,' she said. 'I've got a wedding coming up.'

He'd looked at her with an odd expression. 'I didn't know. Congratulations.'

'Oh, not *my* wedding. Fat chance! I'm married to this place. No, my sister's. She'll kill me if I have to get the dress altered this close to the day.'

'The hours you work I can't see you putting on so much as a centimetre.' His glance skimmed over her trim figure.

'I comfort eat when I'm stressed.'

'Well then, tell me what's stressing you and I'll stand you a skinny latte.'

She sighed. 'It's the Beachams. I'm just not getting them.'

'How d'you mean?'

'There's something bugging the mum. She's sort of ... uneasy, tense, close to the edge.'

Ruaidhri frowned slightly, leaning his elbows on the table. 'Wouldn't you be? Good grief, look what she's contending with.'

'Oh, not about the accident and the organ business. Of

course I understand that. But there's something else going on. Something I can't put my finger on.'

'The old sixth sense, huh? Tell me more.'

'She hardly looks at Mr Beacham. She's positively hostile to the boyfriend. And she's ... I don't know ...' – she spread her hands dismissively – 'jumpy? Furtive almost.'

'OK. And Mr Beacham?'

'Well, at least she's real. But him, he seems to be ... sort of ... buried. Totally buttoned up. You don't get to see the husband, the father, the grandfather. It's like he's detached from the whole thing. He's like a machine, churning out statistics and questions.'

'Safer than emotions, maybe?'

'Maybe.'

'What kind of questions is he asking?'

'Stuff like, would doctors ever take the organs without consent? What would happen if they did? Who decides where the organs go? Who gets on the transplant list? As if he's afraid the organs will go to some unworthy cause.'

'Might they?'

'Depends on your definition of worthy.'

'You're asking a minister of the church that?' he said with a half-smile, but she swatted the attempt at humour aside with a dismissive hand.

'You and I both know that it's all about how ill the recipients are, whether they could withstand major surgery, and their chances of long-term survival. But *he*'s worrying about whether they're gay, or alcoholics, or smokers, or racing drivers, or whatever.'

'Ahhh. That kind of black and unforgivable unworthy.'

'You know what I mean.'

'Course. I'm only winding you up. So what's niggling you?'

'That's the thing. I can't get a handle on what's *behind* his questions. On the surface he's in favour of donating, but it's like he's suspicious of everybody's motives. The latest thing was, out of the blue, "So it's a *medical* decision, then?" said kind of accusingly.'

'And you said?'

'Some parts of the process are medical decisions, certainly. Deciding when a patient's actually dead, that's medical. Deciding who should be a potential recipient, that is too. But deciding whether or not organs may be used for this purpose – well, it's partly family and partly medical. The family say if they agree with donating the organs, but the doctors decide if the organs are suitable for transplanting.'

'Sounds OK to me.'

'But then his next question was, "So, if there was a dispute, would the police or the legal people get involved?" What was *that* all about?'

'Ahhh. I see where you're coming from.'

'And another thing ... Well, see, when I'm talking to you like this, you look at me when I'm speaking, you respond to what I say. Mr Beacham doesn't.'

'I like looking at you.'

Sarah was annoyed to feel colour rising in her neck. It didn't mean anything. 'It's as if he's thinking about something else, a hidden agenda. And I don't know what it is.'

'Maybe he's been reading stuff on the net. Way-out examples of things going wrong.'

'He has too. Stuff coming out of America, with people suing for compensation, things like that. How did you know that?'

He tapped his dog-collar and grinned at her. 'Hot line!'

She couldn't help laughing. 'You're incorrigible. You sure you didn't buy your divinity degree?'

'What divinity degree?'

'Speaking of the internet,' she said, 'did you know that a Chinese teenager sold his kidney to buy an iPhone and iPad?'

'You're kidding!'

'No. Seriously. The illegal surgery nearly killed him too. Read it somewhere reliable.'

'Well, when I get called in in the early hours in future I guess I'll hang onto my kidneys instead of my wallet. Probably worth more.'

'Probably,' she nodded. 'You've spent time with the Beachams, did you notice anything odd?'

'Me? Can't say I did. But they've had a fiendish wallop

of bad luck, haven't they? They've already lost a baby – ah, you didn't know about that?'

She shook her head.

'Long time ago. But the son-in-law died more recently too. Now they've lost a daughter and a granddaughter. Suddenly, tragically. Their security's shot to pieces. They can't trust anyone or anything. They're both grieving in their own way, but as you know, couples tend to take it in turns to fall apart. Maybe it's just not his turn yet. Maybe he feels he has to hold it together for both of them, be the strong one.'

'Could be.'

'Besides, it's not over yet. Hard to let themselves mourn at the moment, with the daughter still here, and the other wee girl needing them to be there for her too.'

'Fair enough. Maybe I'm reading too much into it.'

Before Sarah could continue, someone moved between them. It was Oliver Reynolds, but a different Oliver from the one she'd seen before, hesitant, almost apologetic.

'Excuse me interrupting, but am I allowed to talk to you? I know I'm not actually related to Ellie but ...'

'Course you can.' Sarah was instantly on her feet. 'Come to my office, it's quieter there.' She turned back to Ruaidhri. 'Thanks for the chat. And the latte. Text me later?'

'I will indeed.'

She gave Oliver time to settle himself with a glass of water before she spoke. She couldn't help noticing he was a strikingly handsome man, even in grief. Classic profile, thick curls, absurdly long dark eyelashes.

'Now, how can I help you?'

The restless movement of his hands on the glass told its own story, but the nails were carefully manicured, the skin soft.

'Transplants are common nowadays, aren't they?'

The intense gaze was focused on her. Concentrate, Sarah.

'Relatively, yes. Compared with a few decades ago anyway.'

'Problem is, there aren't enough organs to go round, right?'

'That's right.'

'And it's expensive doing it, yeah?'

'Ye-es.'

'But if you get a transplant, that's a once-and-for-all cure?'

'Not necessarily.'

'No?'

'It isn't always successful. Sometimes the organ fails. Sometimes it needs to be replaced further down the track. And in any case the patient needs to take drugs to stop rejection ... I'm not sure where you're going with this.'

'I suppose what I'm asking is, you people in here, you aren't casual about transplants, are you?'

'Certainly not, no. A huge amount of care and work and thought and planning goes into every single one of them.'

'So it makes the organs kind of precious.'

'Very.'

'See, that's why I'm having a hard time with all this shilly-shallying. The organs are precious. There are folk out there desperate for them. You all take this stuff seriously. Time's running out. I mean, why hang around? Don't get me wrong, I know it's tough on Ellie's parents and everything, but it's what *she* wanted. It's *her* organs. It's there in black and white – she signed the register. She *told* me that's what she wanted. Surely ...' He spread his hands in despair.

'I know, it's hard. I sympathise. But we really do need to have the family on board too. We have to ask lots of questions; they wouldn't be able to deal with that if they weren't onside. And sometimes they just need time.'

'I don't get it. I mean, her mother – you'd think she'd be *glad* to have something of Ellie living on, wouldn't you?'

'Maybe. And in time she might come to feel like that. But once she agrees, she's acknowledging that Elvira really is dead. While she procrastinates, she can still visit her, see her, touch her. Almost tell herself, Elvira's still alive. She's not, of course, but to her mum she can seem to be.'

'It's just dragging things out. We can't arrange anything.

We can't sort things out. We can't *move*.'

'I know.'

'And seeing her, touching her ...' Suddenly the façade crumbled. Sarah reached for a fistful of tissues and slid them into his hand. She placed one hand tentatively on his back and sat quietly beside him, waiting.

Eventually Oliver took a quivering gulp of air. 'Sorry. Sorry. Don't know what came over me. It's the first time ...'

'It's OK. It's natural. No need to apologise.'

'It's so damnably hard. While she's physically there, with us, it's like being in a hellish time-warp. Can't go back, can't go on.'

'I know.'

'And then there's Willow. She hates me. I'm an intruder, trying to take her daddy's place. I'm not – trying to take his place, I mean, but she sees it that way. And now ...' He stopped abruptly and again closed his eyes against the pictures in his mind.

'And now?' she prompted eventually.

'Now she'll blame me. It was all my fault.'

'How come?'

'It was me who delayed her mother, made her late for the dance class. That's why she had to speed.'

For the next quarter of an hour Sarah listened and did her best to comfort a man whose world had just been torn apart, whose conscience was wracked with guilt. It seemed to calm him sharing the chaos in his head.

'Thanks for listening. You're good at what you do. Don't know how you can bear it, though.'

'Thanks.'

'What you said about it being a gift of love? It's a weird notion of love.'

'D'you think?'

'Maybe we ought to pay folk for their bits.'

'There are committees debating that very thing.'

'Doesn't seem quite kosher, does it,' Oliver grimaced.

Sarah half smiled. 'We Brits do prefer altruism, it's true.'

'D'you think we should change to an opt-out system, like they say?' he asked.

'That's a tough question. Ideally we'd all like people to give their organs freely and willingly, but there are those who argue that the desperate shortage of organs trumps finer feelings.'

'But if folk *know* that an opt-out system operates ...'

She mimed a swinging balance.

'You prefer it all open and above board, and not by default?' he suggested.

'Something like that. For me personally, there's always going to be that niggle that says, did they *really* consider this? Are we presuming consent where they'd decline if they were asked directly? Although it has to be said, research shows that far more people say they agree with donation than get around to joining the register. That's a frustrating statistic for us in this business. So I suspect my heart is ruling my head on this, which isn't terribly clever.'

'Don't know about that, but one thing I do know, I'm going on that donor register. Today. Should have done it years ago, but somehow I just never got round to it.'

'Easily done. We always think there's plenty of time.'

'Until something like this happens. And then you realise.'

'Exactly.'

Chapter 13

Willow

OUCH, THAT HURT.
    What's that humming noise? …

I can smell … don't know. Something funny …

Who are these people? I can hear voices. Why are they
swimming under water … ?

Is that …? … Granny? What's she on about?
    Where's Mummy? I want Mummy …

I need a drink.
        Is it night-time? Why can't I open my eyes?
        Am I dreaming?
        I don't like it …

Grandpa? Reading … What's it called? I know it …
        Ahhhhh …

'Wake up, Willow, please, darling. Wake up for Granny.'

Granny?

'Nurse, come quickly! Look. Her eyes. There was a flutter. There was!'

'Hi, Willow. Can you open your eyes for me? Look, your Granny's here.'

That light's too bright. It hurts.

'Oh, Willow, you're waking up. Hello, sweetie. It's Granny. Can you see me?'

'Willow. I'm going to hold your hand. I want you to squeeze my fingers if you can hear me. OK? Squeeze.'

I squeeze.

'Oh, well done. Well done.'

'She did? She can hear? She can understand?'

'She squeezed my fingers anyway. Well done, Willow. I'll let the consultant know, Mrs Beacham. He should be round soon.'

'Oh, thank God,' Granny says. 'Thank God.'

Why is she crying? Grannies don't cry.

I'm so tired ...

Chapter 14

Carole

I STROKE THE HAIR back from Ellie's face. I've always loved her hair, so much nicer than my nondescript mouse or Guy's brown. Where did this stunning red come from?

It's good this, being alone with her, no watchful eyes waiting for me to fall apart. Talking to her, nobody listening. But it won't last. They need time with her too.

'Before your dad gets back, I need to explain, Ellie. You do understand, don't you, sweetheart, that I can't let them take all your precious organs? I can't. You do see that, don't you? I daren't. Just think. Other people ... strangers ... walking around with bits of you inside them ... Would they feel your feelings, d'you think? Would they somehow peep into the cupboards of your mind, see our family skeletons? How can we be sure? How can anybody know? There're plenty of people out there saying they changed, once they had a transplant. Got new tastes, new memories.

'When I came back in just now, saw you lying there so peacefully, it made me even more sure. That's what I want to remember. You're still my Ellie, only now, nothing, nobody, can hurt you ever again.

'You're so special – you always were. Special and different.

'You weren't a pretty baby and you were never contented. Difficult to explain what it was about you. You were ... furious, somehow. You screamed for most of the first six months. But you were the little girl I'd longed for, I could

buy pretty, frilly clothes, dream of one day sharing girly secrets, going shopping together, being best friends.

'And then you were a schoolgirl, growing up – the tantrums, that pouting lip, slammed doors. Oh, the battles we had.

'Poor Ellie, life was never easy for you, was it? Not with that temper, that sharp tongue. Of course, I know it was your insecurity, but my word, you could be hurtful at times. Remember? You always reckoned I loved the boys more. I didn't. I really didn't. It was only that they were less complicated than you, less challenging, less confrontational.

'But then ... remember your wedding day? What a beautiful bride you were, and so happy. And you moved me to tears that night, your arms around my neck, promising me that you might have changed your name but you hadn't changed allegiance, you were still my little girl. Bless you for that, sweetheart. You were, and you still are. You always will be.

'And then Willow came along. Willow. You all over again! Same glower, same fury. Looking as if she'd explode with indignation. You told me you understood now what I'd felt. Bless you, darling, you thanked me for persevering with you. But you've coped brilliantly, Ellie, so much better than I did. I guess you understand her. I've been so proud of you.

'When Maddie was on the way, I must confess – and I can tell you this now – I dreaded another Willow. But Maddie was Drew all over again, placid, easygoing, so contented and affectionate. Your reward.

'Oh, Ellie. After all you've been through, all the heartache, how could something like this happen to you? What's the point of it all?'

I reach out with a shaking hand. Her curls feel exactly as they always did. Her cheek? Cooler perhaps, but otherwise the same soft contours. The whisper of breath is warm on my hand as it puffs out ... out ... out ... exactly in synchrony with the ventilator. I squeeze her hand. The shape is familiar, but her fingers don't respond. There's no quick look, no sudden smile acknowledging my presence, not even a frown. Nothing.

Has the real Ellie gone? My beautiful, capricious, volatile, complicated Ellie. Is she no more?

How can I be sure?

'Ellie ... are you ... you know ... are you in there, somewhere? They say you're not, but I have to be sure. Sure that you are totally ... irrecoverably ... gone. I can't say the other word. Not if there's even the remotest possibility that you might be there at some level, listening.

'How can I go on with a huge Ellie-shaped void where you used to be? No hopes, no future, only memories.

'So many wonderful memories, darling, precious secret reminders that only a mother remembers. You weeping over a dead sparrow. You beating your little fists against my chest when I dared to go out one evening without telling you beforehand. You getting a D in your physics Higher because you flatly refused to apply yourself to something so "useless". You dyeing your long hair black because "red is so uncool, Mum". You confiding that you'd almost stolen an expensive lipstick "just because it was there; just because I could have". You accusing me of ... No. I won't go there. I won't. I know you didn't really mean it.

'You insisting your old mum must be the first to know about the pregnancy. You trusting me more than anyone else to take care of your precious girls.

'So why, Ellie? Why didn't you tell me about Oliver? Why did you talk to him about your organs, and not me?'

I mustn't reproach her. Not now. She must have had her reasons.

I can't cry any more. I feel numb. Must be defensive, I guess. Please let it last. Please don't let me feel anything, ever again.

The rational bit of me knows really: Ellie would be better off dead – properly dead, I mean. She has to be. Two reasons.

Because this isn't Ellie. Even if she survived that brutal crash, she wouldn't be the same Ellie. You can't take part of a car out of somebody's head, damage them so severely inside, and leave them unchanged. Although, if everything else had been OK, we'd have loved her, cared for her, made a life for her.

But more importantly, because her fragile self-esteem would never have coped with the knowledge that it was her speeding that wrecked the future of her two girls.

'*You would have been devastated, totally destroyed. It's better this way, for you.*

'*But can I cope, Ellie, if I thwart your last wish? Will it haunt me for ever? Will they all hate me? Willow. The boys. Dad?*'

Chapter 15

Lennox

LENNOX SLID THE BALLET shoe carefully into the evidence bag. Poor kid, no call for it now, but the grandmother might like it.

He was heading for the hospital anyway to talk to some jerk who'd put in a complaint of harassment against one of his officers. Reckoned the PC had intimidated him, forcing him to speed; that's why he'd crashed into somebody's front garden, demolishing a brand new extension worth easily fifty thousand. Creep didn't seem to realise that a blood alcohol level of 725 told its own story.

The rain lashing on his windscreen turned the hedges to a soft blur of green, the colour of the grinning frog sprawling on the end of Nicole Maggie's cot. He smiled.

His radio crackled but he ignored it, swung right. He parked in the hatched area. Nobody'd challenge a squad car.

The lividly bruised figure in the end bed wasn't so chirpy now. Three broken limbs meant he wouldn't be going anywhere any time soon and he looked like he'd had an unsuccessful encounter with a bulldozer. Morphine had dulled the worst of the pain but nevertheless he grimaced every time he moved.

'Well, Harper, you back to plague me?' Lennox said mildly. 'Your nice little blossoming friendship with AA didn't last then?'

'T'were 'im. Your bloke. 'E were doing seventy easy,' the patient said with a sullen frown, his Yorkshire accent slurring through the painkillers. 'What choice 'ad ah?'

'So if my man was doing seventy chasing you, you must have been doing that or more,' Lennox countered calmly.

''E forced me. Blinded me wi' 'is lights.'

'You training to be an idiot as well as a drunk now, huh? He was flashing at you to stop.'

'Tha' were nowhere to pull up.'

'Only wonder is you didn't kill yourself outright,' Lennox said, shaking his head. 'Thank God the owners were out or who knows what carnage you'd have been responsible for? Shall I tell you exactly what speed you were doing when you hit that wall?'

Harper shrugged.

'Seventy-seven miles per hour. Seventy-seven. In a built-up area. Yards from a primary school.'

The man turned his face away.

'The police car was monitoring you, and the cameras caught you at the end of that road, and witnesses put you in the Thistle and Duck for easily six hours, drinking solidly, they say. Only nobody knew you were into stealing cars as well.'

The man didn't move.

'Not much of a leg to stand on, eh, Harper? Pardon the pun. Evidence stacked a mile high.'

Howard Harper feigned sleep.

'Still want to sign a complaint form?' Lennox asked softly, close to his ear. He waited a beat. 'Nah, didn't think so. Cretin.'

ICU was quiet compared with the ward he'd just left.

The sister at reception filled him in, then listened to his request in silence.

'Thanks, Inspector. I'll see what she says.'

He watched her pad quietly across to a screened-off bed, saw the middle-aged woman look up, flinch, glance in his direction. The nurse returned.

'She'll be with you in a moment.'

The woman leaned over the bed, said something, then moved towards the door. Her eyes were red-rimmed, her skin the colour of ashes. He couldn't help but notice her crumpled shirt and the faint odour of yesterday that clung to her.

'Mrs Beacham?'

She nodded, eyeing him warily.

'My name's Inspector Lennox McRobert, ma'am.' He showed his identification, but she scarcely even glanced at it. 'Sorry, don't want to intrude. Shall we?' He indicated the corridor.

Not until she was safely seated did he continue. 'I'm so sorry for your loss. Terrible business. Must be desperate for you.'

She blew her nose hard.

'I was at the scene of the accident and ...' he began.

Her eyes dilated. 'You saw ...'

'Oh, no, sorry, I wasn't the officer in charge. I was just ...' Just what? An observer? Checking up? Escaping the office? 'I was present when the emergency services were attending to your daughter and the girls. And afterwards ... I saw ... well, I've brought something that I thought you might want to keep.'

He hesitated before placing the shoe on her lap.

She stared down at it. Then she picked it up and held it tightly to her chest, rocking back and forth, her shoulders heaving, tears coursing silently down her cheeks.

'Maybe I shouldn't have ...' Lennox stammered.

'Oh no. Thank you for bringing it. It's just that ... well, she ... Willow ... so much loved ... her dancing.'

The past tense said it all. Lennox felt a lump too big to swallow.

Eventually he broke the silence. 'If we can help in any way ...'

Carole's voice was muffled in her hanky. 'Could you ... the police ... keep the press away? Make them leave us alone?'

'We can try. Your Family Liaison Officer will ...'

'It's only ... I don't want Willow ... reading things. Blaming her mother.'

'I should think they've printed all they will about the collision. Unless anything comes out at the inquest that they don't already know.'

Again there was that haunted look he'd seen when she first saw him.

'Inquest? There'll be an …?'

'OK. Let's leave it at that.' The voice came from behind him. 'Thank you, Inspector. I can't imagine the press will be remotely interested in us.'

Lennox stood up. The man, who moved to stand slightly in front of Mrs Beacham, was a couple of inches shorter than Lennox, but holding his gaze sternly.

'Guy Beacham. Elvira's father.'

'Mr Beacham. I was just returning something of your granddaughter's from the scene of the accident. Didn't mean to intrude.'

'No, you weren't,' Carole fluttered. 'Thank you. You've been very kind.'

Lennox inclined his head slightly towards her. 'Hope your wee girl goes on all right.'

Back in his office he drummed his fingers on the edge of his desk. What was bugging him? Vague bells. A policeman's instinct, that's all, nothing tangible … Something about that encounter with the Beachams …

He swung round and tapped letters into the search engine.

ELVIRA KENNEDY.

Yes, there was the incident. He read every word slowly. Nothing jumped out at him.

KENNEDY. BEACHAM.

BEACHAM. CAROLE. GUY. ELVIRA.

He kept playing with words, scanning the results.

His attention was suddenly arrested.

His eyes flickered over the details, reading, re-reading. Must be the same family. Must be. No wonder the mother'd startled when he appeared in uniform. So that's why the husband shut her up.

And of course, that was the distant bell. The name. Elvira.

'Thanks, Maggie,' he whispered.

He drove straight back to the hospital. His luck was in; Carole Beacham was on her own in the foyer buying a hot chocolate.

She shrank back when she saw him.

'Sorry. No need for alarm. Only came to reassure you really. Most unlikely anything from the past will come out. Shouldn't imagine anybody'd dig around in the first place, not for a regular traffic collision. And with the married name and everything, pretty difficult to join up all the dots even when you try to.'

She stared at him. 'You … know?'

He nodded. 'Safe with me, though, ma'am.'

'How?'

'Policeman's instinct. Looked it up. Name rang vague bells too. Elvira. Unusual. I helped somebody years ago with a study about … well, cases … like yours. Sorry.'

'Who else …?'

'Nobody s'far as I'm concerned. And new name, new place, old news – no reason why it should get out.'

Tears filled Carole's eyes. 'She's been a brilliant mother. I'd hate for Willow to think … Specially now she's gone.'

'Absolutely. One less thing to worry about, I hope.'

'Thank you. Thank you for that,' she whispered.

'No problem. Good luck.'

Lennox wondered if he had a duty to tell the Beacham's Family Liaison Officer. But such old news had no bearing on the current case, surely. No, he'd keep it to himself, at least meantime. These people deserved a bit of privacy.

He was soon immersed in the usual welter of paperwork. Made him wish he hadn't taken promotion. Out there, in the real world, on the front line, battling crime, that's where he'd been happiest, coming home to Maggie and the kids.

Chapter 16

Oliver

CAROLE SEEMED TO BE avoiding him. When he followed her out of Ellie's room ... well, north face of the Eiger about summed it up.

'Please, a few minutes?'

'For?' She kept on walking.

'To explain?'

She paused. A public corridor wasn't ideal but this was probably all the encouragement Oliver was going to get.

'When I first met Ellie, Drew was still alive. She needed a friend back then, an uncomplicated friendship, somebody to lean on, somebody to talk to. Somebody who wasn't emotionally involved in what was happening to Drew. And that's when she first told me how she felt about organ donation. She'd have wanted an organ for him if it'd been possible, so she reckoned the least she could do was offer hers.'

'That was then.'

'But afterwards, when we were ... *together*, she said I ought to know she meant it. Just in case.' When Carole didn't respond he ploughed on. 'We were talking about that bit in the application for a driving licence where it says, d'you want to register or don't you?'

'And?'

'She said it was a step in the right direction, but people needed to be properly informed about the whole process – removing the organs, matching, all that kind of thing – talk about it and understand how everything works, realise they can choose which bits they give.' Oliver broke off, his voice unsteady. He took a deep breath. 'Look, OK, you know Ellie. It wasn't a nice quiet rational discussion, I admit that, not when it started. She was mad. Ranting, right?'

'What about?'

'About the mix-up when the DVLA changed over to a new computerised system. Apparently the boxes for giving different things – heart, corneas, liver and stuff, got moved around. Something like that.'

'That's Ellie.' It was so soft he wasn't sure she'd meant him to hear it.

'But it led into her making sure I knew it was what she wanted. She was fierce about it. Got me to promise. "They can have the lot," she said.'

Carole looked away from him, fidgeting with the cuff of her sleeve. 'The lot? No ... no limits at all? No conditions?'

'*She* wanted them to take everything. *I* was the one with limits.'

Carole held her breath.

'I pleaded with her, not eyes. Please.'

It was too much for both of them. Oliver guided her into a side corridor where three chairs were stacked. She leaned onto the top one and wept.

Eventually she managed a choked, 'You've been with her for a few months ...'

'Yes, and I know it's nothing compared with the thirty-five – almost thirty-six – years, you've had. I understand that.'

'But you think you can speak for her better than me, her mother.'

'No, I don't, but I happen to know what she thought about *this*. And she made me promise. She cared passionately about people – about Drew and the beastly time he had with his cancer, about her kids. Even when they played up, she was always on their side. The best.' Again he had to stop.

Carole nodded but said nothing.

'She was passionate about justice too, people's rights, that sort of thing.'

She was watching him steadily now.

'And I feel so bad about the accident that I need to do *something* to try to salvage some good out of this tragedy.'

'We all feel bad about the accident.'

'No, but it was my fault.'

Carole froze, staring at him. 'But you weren't even there.'

'I was at the house that day. I made her late for Willow's lesson, that's why she was driving so fast.'

'You?'

'Look, you can't blame me any more than I blame myself. I'd give anything ... *anything* ... to put the clock back and do things differently. She didn't know I was coming. I had an appointment with a client in the Borders. I'm in finance – help folk sort out their investments, that kind of stuff, and I travel a fair bit. I had a couple of hours to kill, so I dropped in on the off chance.' Oliver closed his eyes. The image of Ellie's welcome was so vivid. She'd been in the shower, only a towelling robe between him and bliss. The feel of her body, the touch of her hands, it was all so immediate ... so real ...

He swallowed hard. 'Maddie hadn't woken up from her afternoon nap, so I stayed with her while Ellie went to collect Willow from school. They did her homework and everything, exactly like they always do, and I kept my distance, because ...' Oliver broke off abruptly and shot a wry look at Carole. 'You might as well know, Willow resented me, and she didn't make any secret about it. She didn't like Ellie spending time with me. We tried, we really did try, both of us, to make sure Willow had quality time with her mum as much as possible. Especially after school.

'Anyway, later Ellie started to get ready for taking Willow to dancing. She went up to wake Maddie. I followed her and well, we just stopped to have a kiss and ... we were fooling around a bit, and that delayed her a few minutes longer, so she was late setting off. Willow was not a happy bunny, and Ellie was really getting it in the neck about how she was always breaking her promises and everything. So I guess inside she must have been wound up. I mean, *I* was, and I wasn't having to drive with all that whining and everything ...' He broke off suddenly. This was Carole's precious granddaughter he was maligning, her almost *dead* granddaughter, her sole remaining shred of Ellie.

'I'm sorry. She's only a kid and she misses her dad. And it wasn't her fault, it was mine. I shouldn't have delayed Ellie. Willow was right, her mum *did* promise to get her there on time. It was all my fault.'

'We all do things we regret.'

But mostly they don't end in tragedy. It hung between them unsaid.

'I am desperately, desperately sorry.' Oliver gritted his teeth. 'Mrs Beacham, you have to know, I loved your daughter. I wanted her to marry me. She knew that, but she wouldn't agree to anything until Willow came round to the idea. And she wanted more time, she wanted to be sure. Marriage was for life, she said.'

Carole seemed to recoil. When she eventually spoke her voice sounded sharp. 'But … I didn't know anything about you.'

'I'm sorry about that. It wasn't my doing. I wanted the world to know how I felt about her, but her girls came first with Ellie. It was part of the deal. I didn't always like it, but I was under no illusions.'

'That's Ellie,' Carole said so softly again Oliver felt it wasn't meant for his ears.

'Donating her organs – it figures. It was part of Ellie's drive to help everybody who needed helping. You probably know she befriended all the local *Big Issue* sellers. And if she noticed anyone looking sad or neglected she was in there, listening, sympathising, cheering them up. She really cared. And she wouldn't want her last opportunity to help to be wasted, she really wouldn't. That's what I came to say. I'm truly sorry if it makes things harder for you, but she'd slaughter me if I didn't a least *try* to make her voice heard.'

'Oh, I think you've done that.'

'Like I said to Sarah, the transplant nurse, it doesn't make sense to me. I mean, what's the point of deciding for yourself, carrying a card, being on the register and everything, if they don't take any notice when you're dead? Why bother? It would have made Ellie so mad, she'd be in there fighting, if she knew.'

'And what did Sarah say?'

'She said they try to send out a strong message that you should talk to your family, make sure they know you really mean it, it's not up for negotiation.'

'And it seems Ellie did talk ...' – a gulp caught her words and twisted them – 'only not to me.'

'Honestly, I don't think it was intentional. You know Ellie. It probably never *occurred* to her you'd object. She was so used to standing on her own two feet. She was an adult, a mother herself, so it was up to her. And besides, do any of us really think it'll happen to us? Not for years anyway. She probably thought – if she thought about it at all – that you wouldn't be around to mind ... well, you know what I mean. Mostly we don't outlive our kids, do we?'

'Thank God.'

'I'm sorry. I didn't mean to rub it in. I was only trying to ...'

'I know. I know.'

'And when she was married, well, it'd be down to Drew to agree ... or not, as the case may be. She probably told him.'

'And that would have passed to you if she'd accepted you.'

'I guess so.'

'So perhaps she was closer to saying yes to you than you realised.'

'Maybe. Nice idea anyway. But I don't think Ellie worked like that. She talked, about anything, everything. She let me know what she was thinking: what riled her, what comforted her, what she wanted out of life. That was just the way it was.'

'Thank you.' It was barely above a whisper.

'What for?' he asked cautiously.

'Giving her that. Being there for her, loving her like that. Fighting for her now.'

'I should be thanking you for having such an amazing daughter. She was a one-off. And I can't bear to think ...' Tears choked the rest of his sentence.

Carole looked away. Indeed, how could any of them

bear this loss?

When he'd eventually regained control, Oliver sounded more brisk than he intended. 'I reckon it's the least we can do now.'

Carole drew in her breath sharply. 'I need to talk to Guy. It's our decision.'

And with that she abruptly walked away back to Ellie's room without him.

Oliver leaned against the chairs heavily. It was one thing being Ellie's champion against opposition to her will, but the reality of what he was advocating horrified him. Graphic pictures flashed through his brain now, pictures gleaned against his better judgement from the forensic medical dramas Ellie was addicted to, the post-mortems ...

Bodies laid out on steel benches, obscenely naked. Policemen, detectives, ghouls, watching in the gallery. Hearts, lungs, livers, lifted out of bloody cavities, weighed on steel scales. Raw recruits fainting at the smells. Body fluids under the microscope. Curious eyes seeing evidence, piecing together events leading up to the death, seeing, knowing, commenting, recording. They'd know ... his DNA was everywhere.

He gave himself a shake. He wasn't on trial here. OK, he'd admitted his culpability to Carole, but to the police, the doctors, it was a simple accident: a young woman driving too fast for the road conditions. They saw it all the time. She was another statistic, another source of fresh, healthy organs that could save lives. And she wouldn't be exposed on a steel table, she'd be in an operating theatre, decently draped, far away from prying eyes, dignity and respect for her altruism uppermost. Getting what she wanted.

He could hear her voice still: 'Promise me. Promise me. I'm not letting you out of here until you do.' She'd straddled him, pinning him to the sofa with those long legs, both hands pressed to the sides of his face so he couldn't avoid her demands, couldn't be diverted by more base emotions.

'OK, OK. I promise. But for goodness' sake, let's talk about something happier than your blooming death.'

She'd instantly softened and allowed him new liberties with her body ...

Oliver dropped his head into his hands and let out a groan.

Chapter 17

Ruaidhri

RUAIDHRI CAMERON MADE his way slowly round the orthopaedic ward. He kept it light, restricting himself to superficial chat about families or the reason that had brought the men into hospital, but on the alert for openings. Very occasionally patients welcomed a quiet prayer – usually the older ladies with a lifetime habit of Sunday morning services under their belts, or a predilection for Aled Jones and *Songs of Praise*.

The face in the end bed was unrecognisable; looked like a horse had stamped on him. 'James Appleton' the nameplate said. 'RTC'.

'You do confesshionssh, Fadder?' the man slurred, bloodied saliva oozing between his wired teeth.

'Sorry, no, but we do have a Roman Catholic chaplain. I could arrange ...'

Appleton grabbed his arm in a fierce grip. 'Dey fitsuss up.'

'It's what they do in here, fix people up.'

'Nah. Nod doctorsssh. Plisssh.'

'You want to speak to the police?'

'Nah. Deir fault. Dey did disssh.' He swept his good arm comprehensively over his many injuries.

'Ahhh. That's a bit outside my area of competence, I'm afraid, Mr Appleton. You should maybe get yourself a lawyer?'

'Huh. Nah use d'loddayu.'

Three beds further along, someone officially labelled 'William Taylor' beckoned him closer.

'See that guy you were talking to in the end bed? Appleton? He's got a bottle in his bed. Reckon the nurses oughtta know.'

'It's OK. They use bottles in here when people can't get to the toilet,' Ruaidhri explained.

'Naaah. Not *that* kind of bottle! You just out of the seminary, mate?'

'Ahh.' Ruaidhri glanced across at the smashed face. Appleton was currently doing his best to tear the drip from his arm.

The nurse he approached was less than appreciative. 'I'm sorry, but we're going like a fair here. Better things to do with our time than stopping Mr blinking Appleton self-destruct for the umpteenth time.'

The chaplain beat a retreat, memories flooding through his brain ... three of his classmates victimising a puny lad with thick glasses and a lisp ... trying to alert their form teacher to the bullying ... being waved away with a terse instruction to 'Man up, Cameron. Fight your own battles. No place for wimps in this school.' He'd been twelve years old. It had been that lack of sympathetic listening that had started him on his own pathway to a career in pastoral care.

Outside in the corridor he found three children engrossed in defacing the posters instructing all visitors to douse their hands in antibacterial solutions, keep their respiratory bugs to themselves, and take all well-intentioned bouquets of flowers home instead of leaving them to kill the current batch of vulnerable patients ... only politely.

'Well, hello, boys and girls,' he began, in his best avuncular tones.

They took no notice.

He reached across to tap the oldest one on the shoulder. The boy who looked about ten, jerked around, batting him away.

'Paws aff, you perv, or ma faither'll hae your baws fa

breakfast.' He made an obscene gesture.

'Steady on, son. Nobody's going to harm you, but you can't go around destroying hospital property like this. Where's your mother?'

'Skidaddled, un't she?'

'And your father?'

The boy jerked a thumb towards the ward Ruaidhri had just left.

'So who brought you here?'

'Wursel. To see our faither.'

Ruaidhri glanced at the notice on the ward door. Visiting didn't start for another forty minutes. A lot of damage could be done in forty minutes.

'Look, you've got a long wait. How about I take you down to the café and get you all an ice cream?'

The second child guffawed. 'Faither tellt us about yous men. Dinnae listen, he says. Nae sweeties, nae bribes, nor nothing. Even if he's got a dug collar, he says. *Specially* if he's got a dug collar. So shove aff, mister.'

Ruaidhri backed away and went in search of a security man, feeling suddenly a lot older than his forty-one years.

The office of the specialist nurse in organ donation was closed but he tapped anyway.

'Come in.'

He inched the door open cautiously, steeling himself for more rejection.

'Anyone in here got time for a battered and beaten waif and stray?'

'Maybe. Depends.' She finished typing something on her computer and then glanced up, a distracted look on her face.

'Apparently I'm a cross between a sucker, a pest, and a pervert today,' he said dolefully. 'Is there the remotest possibility I might be of some scant use to any of the families in your care who are currently contemplating death as a better option than life? I might just be able to identify with them.'

She patted the chair in front of her. 'Tell all.'

He outlined his most recent encounters embellishing

them with absurdly exaggerated gestures.

She grinned. 'Ahh, give me the unconscious ones any day!'

'Or better still, the deceased.'

'Absolutely.'

'So, can you use me anywhere?'

'Well, you could try strolling by ICU, test the vibes, see if the Beachams would talk through their hang-ups to a man who takes his authority from a boss higher up the pecking order than the hospital chief exec.'

'Now there's a challenge,' he said. 'You no further forward on this one?'

'Nope, so nothing to lose. Off you go and work your magic on the Beachams.'

'Bless you, my child,' he intoned, waving his hand in the shape of a cross with a decidedly irreverent look. 'See you later.'

'And don't come back until it's in the bag!' she called after him.

He found both parents sitting with Ellie. The mother looked as if she hadn't slept for a week.

'How're you coping?' he asked gently.

Guy shrugged. 'It's like being in limbo.'

Ruaidhri nodded. 'I know. And Elvira's so young and beautiful. Nothing prepares you for a desperate situation like this.'

'You feel so ... powerless.'

'You do indeed. I really sympathise. I've been in a similar situation myself, and I know how agonising it is.'

'Family member?' Guy asked without looking at the chaplain.

'My mother. We had to make a decision about her organs too.'

'So you *do* know,' Carole whispered.

He nodded.

'What did you decide?' Her look was intense.

'Sadly we couldn't agree. My sister and I wanted to

donate; it was what Mother wanted. But my father was totally opposed.'

'So, what happened in the end?'

'We ran out of time. We couldn't persuade him. The deadline came and went. But listen, I'm not meaning to put pressure on you. It's very much a personal choice. You have to do what's right for *you*. I was only commiserating with the pain and anguish.'

'Thank you for sharing that,' Carole said softly. 'It helps … knowing we aren't alone.'

'That's why I came. You aren't alone. Anything I can do?'

'Thank you, but no,' Guy said emphatically. 'This is our call.'

'Of course. I understand.' Ruaidhri looked across to Carole and gave her a quiet smile. 'I'll be holding you in my thoughts and prayers.'

'Could you …' she hesitated. 'Is it OK to bless her … now, I mean? Now she's …'

'Of course,' he said swiftly. 'As long as your husband has no objection.'

'I'll leave you to it,' Guy said, and left without so much as a glance at his daughter.

Ruaidhri moved towards the bed, placed a hand on Elvira's head, and closed his eyes.

'Father in heaven, thank you for the rich life of this beautiful vibrant daughter and young mother, Elvira. Thank you for all the joy that she has brought to this world. May memories of her smile, her laughter, her presence, live on, bright and enduring, and bring comfort in the dark days that lie ahead. You know the heartbreak and sorrow and uncertainty her family are experiencing today. We ask you to be very close to them at this harrowing time, guide, guard and keep them. And grant, we pray, peace and a rich blessing for this lovely girl whose life has been so tragically cut short. Amen.'

Tears were cascading down Carole's cheek onto the hand she held in both hers. Ruaidhri moved around the bed to put an arm around her.

'I am so, so sorry.'

'She didn't ... deserve this.'

'Of course she didn't. But sadly, in this imperfect world of ours, accidents happen.'

'She wanted her organs to be used.'

'Right.'

'But ...'

He waited.

'D'you think ...' – her voice crumbled – 'something of the person ... is still in the organs?'

'You mean ...?'

'Their thoughts and ... emotions and ... tastes and everything ... their secrets ... would they be passed on?'

Ruaidhri took a swift breath. 'Ahh. Opinions differ on that.'

'But what do *you* think?'

'My own personal opinion? Intellectually, I'd say not. Thoughts, emotions, they're held in specific parts of the brain. When the brain dies those things are lost. But I've listened to recipients of organs who've been categorical about inheriting more than a pump or a piece of tissue. They say things like, they're house-proud now and they never were before the transplant. Or they love pickled onions or sauerkraut now whereas they hated them before. Things like that. And they believe those things came from the donor.'

'But you don't?' she persisted, still not looking at him, her fingers stroking Elvira's hand. 'How do *you* explain it then?'

'I'm afraid I'm an old cynic about a lot of things. My limited brain just can't see how thoughts and memories can be carried in empty lumps of muscle or tissue that have been totally disconnected and thoroughly washed and cleaned and cooled and everything, and that had nothing to do with thinking in the first place. But maybe you should talk to Sarah about all this. She's much better qualified than I am.'

'I'd like to know what *you* think.'

'Well, my own layman's answer is that these changes people report are more likely to be a feature of the illness, and then life after the transplant. Your energy levels, your tastes, things like that, are all affected if you're seriously ill. If you're sick enough to need a kidney transplant, let's say, you'll have been on a restricted diet for years, and been unable to do much in the way of exercise or activities. So once you've got a new kidney, and you recover, you have a new lease of life. You have the energy to zoom around with the old hoover, or kick a ball around a pitch, or take up line dancing. For the first time in ages you can eat normally, so of course your tastes seem to have changed – they *have* changed – you can enjoy a spicy curry or strong cheese or liquorice allsorts or pickled gherkins or whatever. The altered preferences haven't come from the donor so much as a side effect of improved health.'

'But I've read things ...' She didn't continue.

'Me too, and I wouldn't want to take away that idea of something continuing if it was a comfort to the donor's family. There are more things in heaven and earth than this world dreams of. Is it a problem for you?'

She nodded.

'You want it to be true?' he asked softly.

She shook her head. 'I want it *not* to be true. They were *her* ... secrets.'

'Of course; I can understand that. These things are precious and private and uniquely Elvira's.'

She didn't reply but the look on her face was one of utter despair.

'Is there something specific, Mrs Beacham? Would it help to talk about it? In confidence.'

She shook her head again, sending a shower of tears onto her blouse. 'So, you're saying ... you're sure ... they wouldn't be passed on?'

'I really do believe so. Intellectually, dispassionately, it just doesn't make sense.' He lightened his tone. 'If you were using the *brain* now – well, that *might* be a different story. Even then, I doubt it could still hold memories after death. We find it hard enough to remember things we've done a few years ago, don't we, while we're still alive? And they were our own memories.'

The ghost of a smile flicked over her face.

'So, no,' he said. 'I don't believe it. And remember I said

so before I knew what you wanted to hear.'

There was a long pause. Ruaidhri kept very still, watching Carole staring down at her motionless daughter.

Eventually she drew in a long quivering breath. 'We haven't got much time left ...'

'Then you must talk. I'll leave you to it. Don't let it be a "No" by default. And do talk to Sarah again if you want more information. She knows far more about all this than I do. And I've probably already exceeded my brief.'

'No, I asked you. Thank you for being honest with me. You've been really kind.'

'I'll let your husband know I've gone.'

'I'm sorry ...'

'No need. He was perfectly entitled to do what was right for him. But now you need him here to reach a decision, together. I'll continue to pray for you. And for Elvira.'

Guy Beacham was hovering outside and needed no second bidding.

Chapter 18

Carole

CAROLE GLANCED surreptitiously at Guy across their daughter's immobile body. He looked twenty years older, his jaw clenched, brow furrowed. Where was the suave businessman who'd controlled a company, travelled the world, never let a situation beat him, now? But even *in extremis* his face was as inscrutable as ever. It stirred something deep inside her.

'The chaplain was lovely,' she ventured. 'He understands.'

'Good.'

A long pause.

'Time's running out.'

'I know.'

Silence.

'I still think there're lots of reasons why not,' she began again.

'Oh?'

'I want to say this in front of Ellie.' Her voice crumpled and she blew her nose hard before continuing.

Guy waited in silence, staring at the tracing of his daughter's heart, still pumping blood around her dead body.

'She's suffered enough.'

'She wouldn't feel anything now,' he chipped in.

'Look,' she interrupted him impatiently, 'I don't want you to try to knock my arguments down. Everybody thinks they have to do that. Just for once I want to tell you how I feel. It won't be all polished and logically argued, but at least it'll be honest.'

'Fair enough. I'm listening.'

'Hacking into her body – it feels somehow disrespectful. Would she still look like herself ... afterwards, I mean? I couldn't bear to remember her ... mutilated.' She felt something strangling her throat, and swallowed hard. 'It's like desecrating a holy place.'

Guy reached across and smoothed Elvira's hair back from her forehead in a simple tender gesture.

'What if they've made a mistake,' – it was barely above a cracked whisper. 'What if they could get her back? Or they find some miracle medical cure. They're always discovering new things.'

Guy shook his head, but didn't speak.

'And what about us?'

He glanced up swiftly, something almost fearful in his eyes.

'It'd be something else for us to go through. More distress. Don't *we* matter too? Haven't *we* suffered enough already?'

Silence fell, neither looking at the other as they fought their private battles.

Eventually Carole ploughed on. 'Besides, we're still numb from the news. I can't take it in. They tell you in bereavement counselling, it's not the right time to make big decisions.' She paused. 'And what if we regretted it later? What would we tell the gir... Willow?'

After a silence that seemed to stretch beyond them, Guy looked up cautiously.

'Is that it? You've decided?'

'No, that's just the way *I* feel. But we know *Ellie* decided for herself. And right now I feel worse about going against her wishes, denying her the chance to help other people, than about all the things I said just now.'

'So, you'll ... do it?' Guy held his breath.

'If you agree.'

'For both of them?'

'If you think so too.'

'I do. I always have. But what made you change your mind?'

'Ellie. It's what she wanted. And what Oliver said about her. And because ... it sort of makes amends for what happened ... you know ... with Sally.'

He stared at her aghast. 'You aren't serious? You can't be. You *can't* be harking back to that. She was a *child*, for heaven's sake. A *four-year-old kid*!'

'Even so. It was Ellie who ...'

'Have you been secretly blaming her all these years?'

'No, of course not. But if she knew, she'd want to do anything she could to compensate.'

'A life for a life, huh?'

'No. But ...'

Guy shook his head. 'You're a long time forgiving.'

'There's one other thing ...' Tears choked her words. 'When the time comes, will you ... tell Willow ... about her mum ... and Maddie ... and the organ thing?'

'Of course I will. And' – he paused, looking directly at her – 'thank you. I know it's been hard for you, but you've made the right decision.'

'And will you go and find Sarah now? Tell her? I can't ... say it.'

She was lying on the bed cradling Ellie in her arms when Sarah found her. The nurse watched in silence as Carole stroked her daughter's cheek, murmuring softly in her ear. Then she entered the room, placed a hand on Carole's arm and let her wordless sympathy flow.

'Did Guy tell you?'

'He did, but I need to check with you personally. Are you quite, quite sure?'

Carole screwed her eyes tightly against the tears. 'I'm sure,' she croaked. 'And I've promised Ellie. I won't go back on it now.'

Sarah gripped Carole's free hand in both her own. 'Thank you. Thank you *so* much.' Her eyes moved to the bed. 'And thank *you*, Elvira.'

From that moment the team went into overdrive.

The questions felt relentless. Sarah was gentle; she let Carole and Guy work through the lists in silence where she could. Twice she emphasised they were only the sorts of things blood donors were asked, but it still cut Carole to the quick. The range of diseases? – no, no, no, Ellie was perfect, in the peak of health. Did she ever have acupuncture or botox? – no, she was beautiful exactly as she was. The answers only underlined the terrible untimeliness of her death. Has she ever smoked? – not since she tried a smuggled cigarette in the girls' cloakroom aged thirteen and got caught by the headmistress, who summoned her parents, who withheld her pocket money and banned all TV for a month. Ever had sex with a man who had sex with another man? ... and that's when her mother realised Oliver would know the answers better than she did.

That too hurt unbearably.

Chapter 19

Sarah

WITH THE NURSES preparing Elvira for theatre, Sarah dived back to her office.

'Phew, you're in a hurry,' said a familiar voice behind her.

She didn't slacken her stride. 'Yep, the Kennedy donation's going ahead. It's all systems go.'

'Oh,' Ruaidhri said. 'I didn't think you'd crack that one.'

'Oh ye of little faith.'

'Hey, hold on a minute. Biblical quotations are meant to be my territory.'

She grinned. 'No monopoly though, huh? Your wisdom must be rubbing off on me. But why the doubt?'

'You were right. There *is* something else going on with this family. But, look … I don't know how to say this, only … I'm afraid I might have exceeded my brief on this one.'

'How come?' she said, unlocking the door of her office.

'I might just have put a wee bit too much pressure on.'

'Yeah?' She was gathering papers and only half listening.

'I'm afraid I let slip some personal information.'

'Oh?'

'About my own experience, having to make a similar decision for my mother's organs.'

Now Sarah's attention was fully focused on the chaplain. 'I didn't know.'

'No reason why you should. I've never mentioned it to

anyone before.'

'And you said?'

'That I was pro donation. I know, I know. Mea culpa. I shouldn't have. That's why I came to find you, to confess. It's no excuse but the mother looked so wretched, and the father's a bit of a sphinx, so I guess I wanted them to know I understood their agonising. It kind of slipped out. When I realised what I'd said, I bent over backwards to emphasise the decision was always a personal thing, etcetera, etcetera, but even so ...'

'I'd like to hear more about your own experience some time,' Sarah interrupted, 'but right this minute I have a whole host of people gearing up to retrieve and transplant Elvira Kennedy's organs. And if I'm reading you right, you're casting a great big cloud of suspicion over this authorisation form.' She rapped her fingers on the papers in her hand. 'So tell me, precisely what did you say? Do I need to go back to the Beachams and double check?'

'Oh help, no! It won't come to that, will it?'

'I'll know more once I've heard exactly what happened.'

Ruaidhri repeated the relevant part of his conversation, looking decidedly chastened.

'Well,' Sarah said briskly, 'it's unlikely that that, on its own, would have made Mrs Beacham sign anything against her will. She's one determined lady. But I'm going to pop along and satisfy myself that it's their settled wish. Both of them.'

'Should I come? Apologise or anything?'

'Best not,' Sarah said. She shot him a sudden smile. 'And don't beat yourself up, you were only trying to help.'

'I'm so sorry to give you extra work.'

'You can owe me!'

'Shall I ... can I wait here? Till you come back?'

'Sure. Help yourself to a coffee.'

When Sarah reappeared her face was expressionless.

'I've blown it?' Ruaidhri asked, grimacing.

She shook her head from side to side slowly. 'All those

folk out there hanging on to life by the skin of their teeth, packing their bags and bidding farewell to loved ones even as we speak, only to have their last hope cruelly snatched away at the eleventh hour.'

'Oh, don't!' he implored. 'I feel wretched enough already.'

'Then you'll be relieved to know that it wasn't down to you at all, though Mrs Beacham said you were "really, really kind", and I quote. It was actually Oliver who persuaded her. The boyfriend? He's been Elvira's champion from the word go, apparently.'

'Seriously? You're not just saying that to make me feel better?'

'As if! No. It's perfectly true. The authorisation is valid and we're back on track. But you ... you're something else.' She studied him with a wondering look.

'Meaning?' he said cautiously, eyeing her with some misgiving.

'You're so ... so thoroughly *decent*. You didn't need to say anything, nobody would have been any the wiser, but ...' She shrugged.

'I don't deserve that, but thanks.'

'And it's true, Mrs Beacham *was* singing your praises. You probably did help her towards the decision, but in the nicest way, simply by being kind and understanding. So, you can bin that hair shirt.'

'Coming from you, that counts. You spend your life supporting and helping people when they're at rock bottom.'

'We'll celebrate care and compassion – the mushy, unquantifiable elements of our job – together then, shall we?' she laughed.

'Would you?' he said quickly, one eyebrow quirked.

'Would I what?'

'Celebrate with me?'

'Sorry, you've lost me now.'

'Let me take you out – for dinner, a concert, a film, whatever you fancy?'

She stood stock still staring at him.

He took a step back. 'Oh dear, have I just made a

complete fool of myself?'

'Sorry. But did you …?'

'Invite you out on a date? Yes, I did. I've been wanting to for ages, trying to summon up the courage. And I guess I just chose the worse moment possible, huh? And misread the signs completely.'

'No,' she said softly. 'You just made a really difficult day much brighter. Thank you, Ruaidhri.'

'Does that translate as a yes?'

'It does, but – don't take this the wrong way – I absolutely can't spend any more time talking right now. There are a zillion things to do to get these organs from A to B in prime condition.'

'Of course. I'll text you later. I might trot along and find Mrs Beacham. And then I think I'll go and do a little victory dance in the chapel.'

'Isn't that a bit heretical?'

'Well, you're already highly suspicious of my theological credentials, so what the heck!'

When they eventually found time to meet away from the safety of their professional roles, there was a new shyness between them.

The restaurant he'd chosen was at the foot of the Pentland Hills, quiet, dimly lit, and almost empty. They were alone in an alcove festooned with musical instruments.

'Ready to pluck off the wall and fill an awkward moment with a medley of romantic highlights,' he whispered, as her eyes took in the unusual décor.

'Can you play any of these?'

'About well enough to empty the restaurant completely if the need arises,' he quipped.

But as they settled into the intimacy of a meal for two in a secluded place, the conversation became more tentative.

'This isn't right for us at the moment, is it?' Ruaidhri said. 'Shall we skip dessert for now and go for a walk?'

'I'd like that.'

Once outside he took her hand in his and they walked in

silence for several minutes, each savouring the new sensations.

'I'd like to hear more about your mother,' she said, 'if it isn't too painful?'

'No, it's fine. She was an amazing person.' Ruaidhri looked off into the distance. 'Incredibly generous. Loyal. Loving. She was never very robust, though – women's problems, and some kind of auto-immune thing – don't ask me what exactly, I didn't understand it all. But she had a marvellous imagination. The stories she told us when we were kids, the games she invented!'

'She sounds lovely.'

'She was. The best. A one-off. Dad struggled though, with her being ill; he was often impatient with her limitations. He was much harder, old school, macho man.'

'Hence your name,' she said.

'Indeed.' He paused and they walked for several paces in silence. 'But ... well, it was more than that – and this is relevant to what happened. When I was in my teens she found out he'd been having an affair with a girl half his age, not much older than me, in fact! She kept it to herself for ages and I had to drag it out of her when I caught her weeping in the garden. It was so unlike her, I thought maybe she was dying or something. When she did eventually tell me, I was livid. I raged at Mum too, said she shouldn't just take it lying down, but she was typically gentle and forgiving. She took a lot of the blame on herself, being too poorly to be a proper wife. And then she said – I'll never forget it – "One day you'll understand, dear," she said. "Marriage is for life, for better or for worse. I promised, and what's a promise worth if you don't keep to it when hard times come?"'

As if on cue they released hands and slipped an arm around each other.

'They jogged along pretty much as usual after that, outwardly at least. Then, when I was in my late twenties, away from home by this time, she had a bad fall. Dad found her at the bottom of the stairs, unconscious, and her condition just deteriorated. She never spoke again.

'After five days they told us she was brainstem dead. My sister Margot and I were devastated, as you can imagine, but we knew Mum wanted to donate her organs so we raised the subject with the doctors. Dad went ballistic. He was absolutely adamant: *no way!* End of discussion. To us it felt like denying her her dying wish. Margot hasn't forgiven him yet.'

'And you?'

'Well, I confess I struggled for months after the funeral. I kept thinking of all she'd done, forgiving him for the affair and everything, being so loyal to him. But Mum's attitude, her words, kept coming back to haunt me. What's Christian love all about if you can't forgive when times are tough? Maybe Dad had his own personal reasons for doing what he did – I doubt he ever talked to anybody about it, and that's a hefty burden to carry all on your own. And I guess he probably did love her in his own way. Now I'm older I can understand better how constant ill-health must have put a strain on their relationship. So we made a kind of peace.

'Not long afterwards he moved away, and about a year later he got married again. We hear at Christmas time, birthdays, but that's about all. He's made a new life for himself and he's got a new family now – two more boys.'

'So that's why you have a special interest in transplants.'

'That certainly, but it might also possibly have something to do with a certain pretty nurse who works in that department.'

Ruaidhri stopped and turned to cup her face in his hands. Their eyes held. Slowly, simultaneously, they moved until their lips met in a soft kiss.

'I've been wanting to do that for ages,' he murmured.

They stood for a long moment holding one another close before he turned to resume their walk with a brisk, 'OK, enough about me, what about you? Your family.'

'Me? I'm as boring as they come. My parents were both teachers. They worked hard and gave us kids a happy childhood. I've got two sisters, both younger than me. But since I left home I'm afraid I've allowed work to dominate.

'My dad had a stroke four years ago. Left him with poor speech and limited mobility. Mum's brilliant with him but she's not getting any younger; she gets exhausted. The work's relentless when Dad's at home. He goes into respite care every ten to twelve weeks, but even so, I'm not there nearly enough. My youngest sister lives closer, and she does what she can, but that's no excuse for me.' She broke off, twisting a ring on her finger her parents had given her on her eighteenth birthday, not looking at Ruaidhri.

'Your work's very demanding,' he offered.

'Mum and Dad aren't, though; they insist I have to live my own life. But I should be there for them more.'

'It's a tough call.'

She sighed. 'I do wonder sometimes, is it worth it? Not just because of Mum, but for me too.' She paused. 'The job, I mean. It swallows you whole sometimes. And I'm my own worst enemy, I admit that. You probably know already, I'm obsessive, a nightmare on stilts – about most things actually,' she added with an irritated gesture, 'but specially about these families. They'd survive if I went home, other people would be there for them, but I feel *I* have to stay, see them through to the bitter end.'

'And then when you do go home, you carry this burden of sorrow with you?' he said quietly.

She nodded.

'And you're totally wrung out,' he said. It wasn't a question. 'Of course you are. You're giving from the depths of your soul.'

'Which is the kiss of death to my social life, I can tell you, which means I'm relying more and more on myself, and I have a horrible feeling I'm pretty much running on empty.' Her voice quavered slightly and she coughed to disguise it.

He nodded. 'I'm not surprised, although watching you in action nobody'd ever guess. You are exceptionally good at what you do, you know.'

She shrugged.

'You are,' he said. 'But you do work too hard. I prescribe a healthy dose of relaxation and fun. And that's where I *can* help if you'll let me. Hey, look at us! We're supposed to be off duty, getting to know one another as real people, and here we are already talking about work.'

'It's good to *properly* talk to you, though, away from the hospital.'

'For me, too.'

He tightened his arm around her waist. 'There's a lot more I want to say to you, but first there's something much more pressing to attend to. I think this is the moment to warn you about my own health issues. It's my heart, you see. Recently it's begun to miss a beat sometimes.' He paused. 'Strange though, it always seems to coincide with catching sight of a certain young brunette. It's been getting noticeably worse lately, and my ECG tracing goes totally off the scale if she comes close to me, I go all breathless and trembly. And ... when she looks at me ... like that ... well, there's only one treatment that offers any hope ... mouth-to-mouth resuscitation.'

He watched the slow smile spread from her mouth to her eyes and drew her into his embrace.

Chapter 20

Carole

I MUST KEEP BUSY. I must. I can't let myself imagine what they're doing to my beautiful daughter. Guy wants to stay, and see her off to theatre, but I can't bear to. I can't, knowing ...

Sitting with Willow, my imagination runs riot. I wish she'd wake up. No, I don't! I couldn't tell her ... not now. I couldn't face her questions.

She's so motionless and pale. There's been nothing more since that flutter of her eyelashes. The nurses say it's early days, give her time, keep talking. She'll hear us long before she shows signs of consciousness.

I brush her hair as I talk, so much finer, less vivid than her mother's. The static electricity crackles around us.

'Maybe you could help me choose some of Maddie's favourite toys for her, how about that? And when you're better we'll go to visit her.

'And I'll tell you stories about when Mummy was a wee girl. We'll make special albums.

'D'you know, she once had such a tantrum that she kicked a hole in the plaster of her room? Grandpa refused to get it repaired until she'd apologised to me for her bad behaviour. She held out for five weeks on that one. I was fed up seeing the plaster dust crumbling over the floor, but Grandpa insisted. "Leave it. She has to learn." He could be very stern with her sometimes. Only he wasn't there a lot of the time.

'And then there was the time she bit your Uncle Freddie on his ear. Goodness me, how he yelled. She reckoned he'd provoked her by letting her stick insects out, but Freddie maintained she flew at him for no reason. And she did have a terrible temper when she was little. You'll find that hard to believe, won't you? She's been such a lovely patient mummy to you. But it's true, she was a real handful when she was younger.

'I used to dread going to school on parents' evening. It wasn't so much what they said, as what I read between the lines. She wasn't exactly naughty, but she obviously challenged them, with her unusual ideas, her way of seeing things. I don't know where she got it from, certainly not me. I've always been timid and conforming.

'But her friends, they were unusual too. She homed in on the downtrodden, the ones other people ignored. She was always a champion of the underdog, and they sort of became her followers. They were easily led. Oliver says she still ... ahh. Never mind.'

I mustn't deceive Willow, but it's too early for me to start using the past tense. Besides ...

Thoughts of what they're doing over at the Infirmary crowd into my mind. I mustn't ...

'Come on, Willow, wake up for Granny. There are so many things here for you to see: books, games, food, puzzles. People have been so kind. And I'll be here every day, helping you with your exercises, getting you fit and strong again so you can come home.'

My voice falters. Home. With all that that means now. I don't want her to know until she has to, certainly not before she's properly awake.

'And when you're ready to come home, we'll get your bedroom decorated in your favourite colour. And you can have all your new books and animals and games and everything all around you, and I won't make you tidy up all the time. And we'll go shopping together, and have one of those long chocolate ice-creamy drinks you love so much. And I'll teach you to knit, and we can go to the beach every day in the holidays, and I'll take you to the cinema, and the ballet, *and musicals. I've had a look and there are some super shows coming later this year.*

'We'll be fine, Willow, you and me. It'll be like having your Mummy a wee girl all over again. Only this time I'll do better, I promise I will.'

The tears won't be repressed.

Oh Ellie, Ellie, Ellie. Forgive me.

PART 2

PART 2

Chapter 21

Carole

THE GRAVE IS BATHED *in soft light. No flowers to trouble me this time.*

'You should see the cards and letters and messages we've received since you died, Ellie, the lovely things everyone says about you. What a force for good you've been. I'm so proud of you.

'And even now, you're still making a difference. We had another letter today, from the transplant coordinator – no, sorry, they don't call her that – the organ donation nurse, Sarah. I'm going to read it to you to let you know what an amazing gift you've given people. Lives have changed completely because of you. Thank you, darling, for having the courage to do what you did. You were right, I was wrong.

'I wish I could put these letters in with you, beside the painting and your old rag doll. They belong to you, not me. You and Maddie. But of course I can't, so I'm going to read them to you instead.

'The first bit's standard.

How are you? I do hope you are coping and that Willow is progressing nicely.

Because of your courage and selflessness good has come out of tragedy. As you know, we're not permitted to disclose the identities of the donors or recipients, but we are able to pass on certain basic information and the thanks of the families concerned.

'This is the bit, Ellie:

Unfortunately the damage caused by the accident meant we could only use your granddaughter Madeline's heart, liver and bones. Her heart went to a little girl who is now able to run and play like other children her age. Her name is Arianne. Madeline's heart saved her life.

We enclose a card from Arianne herself which, I feel I should warn you, she has addressed to Madeline. We hope this isn't too painful for you.

There is no obligation for you to respond, but if you should wish to communicate with Arianne's family, I can forward anything you send to me.

'And then there's the usual stuff about hoping the hurt will ease in time, etcetera, etcetera.

'The card from the wee girl is homemade, Ellie, covered in pink and purple hearts and flowers. Exactly the kind of thing Maddie used to draw, remember? It broke my heart just thinking …

Enough of this. I promised myself I wouldn't be maudlin.

'You can just see this wee soul sitting far too close to the paper copying letters in her best handwriting. Presumably the mum wrote it out for her first – or maybe even wrote it on her behalf. It doesn't say exactly how old she is, or how clever. Anyway it doesn't matter, it's the thought that counts. She's included lovely little spelling mistakes too, like 'heart' without an e, 'yours' with no u, 'thank you' all one word – one of your pet hates, huh? Just like a tot would. I'll read you what it says.

'She starts off, Dear Madeline. *All very grown up. Wouldn't Maddie have been chuffed to get a proper letter all to herself? But let me read the rest.*

Thankyou for giving me your hart. I love it. Mine was no use. Yors is really good. Now I can go to skool when I'm five. I cant wait.
My Mummy says I must say thankyou every day so I do.
I hope you are well.

Lots of love and kisses,
Arianne
    XXXXX

'Isn't that brilliant? All that effort. "I hope you are well." *So sweet. I guess that bit at least came from Arianne herself. She has no idea.*

'Should I tell Willow about this, d'you think? I don't know. She's so unpredictable. It's almost like she resents Maddie getting attention even now. Your dad thinks maybe she's too afraid to let herself think about you and Maddie too much, so she simply blocks it out.

'The letters are a comfort to me, though, Ellie. And if you knew what happened, years ago – I will get around to telling you one of these days – anyway, if you knew, you'd be even more glad. A little girl lives on because of what you did.

'Thank you, darling. A million times, thank you.'

Chapter 22

Madeline's heart

ROSA COULDN'T HELP smiling. From the riot of pink balloons bobbing above the gate, to the candles on the elaborate confection in the centre of the table, everything shouted celebration.

Two hours to go, then everybody would be here, making a fuss of Arianne Elizabeth Louise. When she was born Ray's mother had sniffed: 'Fancy burdening the wee soul with all those names.' Today though, grandparents would unite without complaint with aunts and uncles, cousins, friends, neighbours, playmates – everybody who had encouraged, supported, protected and cared. Everybody that is, except Ray.

It was still hard to believe. After all the years of disappointment and failure, reconciling herself to a childless future, now here she was throwing a *third* birthday party for her miracle baby.

She crept upstairs and stood in the doorway looking across at the sleeping child. Evidence of her premature birth lingered in Arianne's elongated face, her slightly prominent eyes, her skinny limbs, but in all other respects she was a fairytale in the flesh. Her ash blonde hair was so fine it was almost invisible, the suggestion of veins threaded below her translucent skin the only sign of human habitation. And soon Arianne would melt her heart all over again with that one word, 'Mummy.'

No one knew how much it had hurt when her first recognisable sound had been 'Daa'. Rosa had feigned delight in Arianne's brilliance; not even Ray had guessed what it cost her. But then Ray had never really understood what motherhood meant to her. 'If it happens it happens' was his attitude for the first six years of trying. 'We'll have fun while we wait.' And he was more than happy to keep 'practising'. When it didn't happen he changed to 'Loads of things we can do if we don't have kids.' When her periods suddenly stopped and she thought she was menopausal his brand of comfort became 'Thought you'd be glad to be rid of the monthly hassle.' It wasn't that he was cruel or insensitive, he just had this instinct for seeing the best in every situation. If she'd tried to explain how desperately she needed to be first with their daughter he'd have catalogued her genetic advantages – incubating the baby during pregnancy, giving birth to her, breastfeeding her, staying at home with her – what was a tiny 'Daa' compared with all that?

Arianne stirred and tossed her head several times as if trying to shake off a persistent fly. Rosa held her breath. Was she having bad dreams? Beads of sweat stood on her hairline. Was she sickening for something? Please don't wake yet, get your full sleep so you're sunny all the time. Everybody must go away utterly enchanted.

And they did. Arianne performed to perfection. As a reward for good behaviour Rosa allowed her a dessertspoonful of ice-cream, and one square of white chocolate – her annual excursion into the world of other children, outside the confines of organic purity.

She was put to bed at 6.11pm; eleven minutes beyond the deadline, to allow Nana Hester to finish reading the book about rabbit saying goodnight to the moon. Rosa hadn't realised how slowly her mother-in-law moved these days. She filed the knowledge away against the day when she might need a babysitter – a very big 'if'. It was part of her ongoing risk assessment.

The adults had rallied to her aid. They mopped up dribbles and soiled bottoms; they sorted out spats over toys; they cut up eggy bread and Marmite fingers; they insisted on helping Rosa clear up. Somewhere, a fraction below the plimsoll line of permissible thoughts, she wanted to send everyone away and sit down and cry, it was so exhausting, but she kept her public smile pinned firmly in place and let them put things away in all the wrong places.

By the time the last person left she doubted whether she could even climb the stairs, but she must check on Arianne. It was easily an hour and a half since she'd been able to escape the incessant good intentions. She was four steps up when the phone rang. Too bad. Too late. Try again tomorrow. But something made her return and pick it up.

'Hello. Rosa Churchill speaking.'

'Rosa, hi. Only me. How's my princess? Can I speak to her?'

'She's fast asleep, Ray, and you know I never wake her once she's gone down.'

'Not even on her birthday? She'd surely want to hear from her favourite Daddy on her *birthday*.'

'If I wake her now she'll be up half the night and we'll both be too tired for tomorrow and you know what *that* means.'

'OK. If you say so. How did the party go, then?'

'Fine. It was great. Everybody came. She got enough presents to stock a toyshop *and* a baby boutique. And she was as good as gold all the while they were here.'

'Excellent. Glad to hear you enjoyed it. Sorry I had to miss it, but I'll make sure there are no overseas trips next year at this time.'

'How are things going over there?'

'Fine. So far, so good. Well, you know what the Spanish are like: mañana mañana. Got another big meeting this evening with the sales people but I'm on target at the moment for coming home on Friday as arranged.'

'Right.'

'I'd better go now. Give Arianne a big kiss from Daddy. Oh, and Rosa, best not to ring tonight. Don't want to lose this deal.'

'OK. Good luck with it.'

'Thanks.'

'See you Friday then.'
'See you. Bye.'

Rosa began methodically returning all the dishes to their rightful places, feeling strangely bereft without her customary bedtime call to Ray to look forward to, but he'd made it quite clear; no disturbances. A lot was riding on this meeting tonight. Odd really that so much business was carried out late at night. Surely they weren't at their best at this hour. Well, probably the Mediterraneans were, they had long siestas, didn't they?

Arianne was buried beneath the covers so Rosa left her undisturbed while she went for a soak to relieve the tension in her muscles. Bliss! Aromatic oils, scented candles, soft music … it was almost midnight when she woke, the water cold, the bubbles long-since vanished. For once she didn't even stay to scour the bath. She needed to be relaxed if she were ever to sleep without Ray here to guard the house.

Arianne remained invisible at the bottom of her bed but this time Rosa turned back the covers to carry out her routine night-time check; breathing, colour, temperature, body-tone … Her screams brought Billy Drake from next door running.

It was Billy who dialled 999. It was Billy who urged her to ring Ray. She resisted; no point in interrupting important business. Besides there was nothing he could do. But waiting, endlessly waiting at the hospital, she changed her mind. 1.40am. Surely his meeting would be over by now.

It was chilly standing outside the main entrance clad only in a thin nightie and her winter coat.

'Hello?' The voice was young and unknown and foreign and unmistakably female.

No! She couldn't have … not at this hour … surely not!

'Oh, I'm so, so sorry to disturb you … I must have rung the wrong number by mistake …'

'Ahhh … no, wait! What number were you wanting?' the girl said.

Rosa knew it by heart.

'You're looking for Raymond Churchill?'

117

'Yeeaaas ... Is that the right number? Are you minding his phone while he's in his meeting?'

'You're through to his phone, yes. I'll just go and check for you. Who may I say is calling?'

'Rosa. His wife.'

'Ahh ... right.'

Ray sounded annoyed. 'I thought I told you, don't ring tonight, Rosa.'

'I know, and I wasn't going to, but Ray, something dreadful's happened. It's ...' The image of the pale floppy rag-doll she'd found in Arianne's bed robbed her of the power to continue.

'What now, Rosa? What's happened?'

'It's ...'

The phone was winkled out of her hand.

'Look, mate, this is Billy from next door ... Listen ... Don't be ridiculous ... No, course not ... Listen! No *listen*! We're at the hospital ... No, she's all right ... well, as all right as you'd expect. It's Arianne. She's sort of collapsed ... Don't know ... They think it's something to do with her heart, but they're still doing tests ... What, at this hour? ... Suit yourself, but Rosa could do with you here ... It's nothing. Only being a neighbour.'

He handed the phone back to her.

'Ray?'

'I'll be there on the first flight I can get. You hang in there till I get back. She'll be OK. Trust me.'

'Oh.' What else was there to say? 'Bye.'

It was Billy who gripped her hand hard when they told her the tests showed Arianne's heart was enlarged. Was it the premature birth? Was it because she was an older mother? Was it all the excitement of the party? Was it the chocolate?

It was probably caused by a viral infection. Viral? How could Arianne have got anything viral? Everything was sterilised. Everything was organic. Nobody came near her with a sniffle or anything remotely hostile. Rosa had taken every precaution possible to protect her precious daughter for all her thirty-six months of life. And the six months before that.

'We'll put her onto a machine. It'll do the work, give her damaged heart a rest.'

'And then she'll be fine, once she's had a wee rest? We can go home in the morning?' Back to their safe cocoon, away from all the things that might harm her, away from the MRSA and streptococcus, the klebsiella and pseudomonas, and …

They tried to spell it out to her but Rosa had been through too much to think of motherhood being snatched away again. Not while she lived and breathed. She had fight enough for two.

It was a very different Arianne who lay inert in Paediatric Intensive Care from the pre-birthday girl Ray had kissed goodbye to five days earlier. The doctors who came to listen to her chest and gaze at her X-rays were getting more and more senior, their smiles now wafer thin.

They drip-fed information: Arianne was on a ventilator … condition serious … heart failing … going to try to get a Berlin heart … an artificial machine to pump her blood for her … try to keep her alive … until a real heart becomes available … serious shortage … another child has to die … the parents will have to …

That's when she cracked. She and Ray had made that heart. A new one wouldn't be the same. She wouldn't be *their* Arianne, she'd be partly someone else's.

How could they sign permission for surgeons to stop their little girl's heart, rummage around, take out the very thing that made her a living child, sew in another one, a real heart chopped out of somebody else's child, making *them* dead too … very dead … too dead to ever recover. Maybe Arianne would get better, but how would she react to having a foreign heart? To drugs … imagine Arianne having *drugs*! To needing another heart when she was fifteen. These borrowed organs didn't last for ever, not like the original thing, so if Arianne was to stand a chance she'd need lots of other children to die …

Oh, it didn't bear thinking about. Children. Dying. But

then, neither did losing Arianne.

The child continued to cling to her semi-detached life.

Friday.

Saturday.

Sunday.

Monday.

Tuesday.

Wednesday.

Time continued to beat out its own rhythm, a deceptive metronome for Arianne's life.

Rosa continued to pray. Unceasingly.

And on Thursday the machine that would take the pressure off Arianne's failing heart arrived. She looked so tiny on the trolley taking her to the operating theatre, Rosa clinging to her arm right up to the last moment. The nurses had to disengage her fingers one by one, remove her bodily, shutting the door on her anguish. Her body slithered down the wall at precisely the same time as noxious fumes entered Arianne's unsullied lungs, before knives and needles seared into her perfect skin, gloved hands violated her innocent body.

Rosa sat immobile in the corridor for the whole of the time it took them to connect Arianne to her only hope. Her unconscious form seemed even more fragile by the time they brought her into the recovery room and Rosa could tie the umbilical cord tightly to her again. The nurses told her Arianne would sleep for some time; it was best for her; the operation had gone as well as could be expected; but still Rosa called her name, softly at first, then more urgently. She had to come back. She *had* to.

Ray came and went. He couldn't 'sit there doing nothing' all day; best he went to the office, 'kept on top of stuff.' She could ring him any time; he'd come straight away. But work would 'keep his mind off things.'

Rosa said nothing.

Three days after the Berlin heart took over keeping Arianne

alive, she finally managed, 'Mummy?'

The staff kept sounding alarm bells ... very sick ... weakened state ... a match might not become available in time ... but Rosa closed her ears and concentrated all her energy on willing her daughter through each heartbeat.

Fifteen days after the Berlin heart began beating out Arianne's rhythm of life, a red Fiat was crushed by an orange Sainsbury's lorry and Madeline Kennedy's perfect little organ became surplus to requirements.

Cardiac surgeon Rheinhold Valfrid stood back from the table. 'Off bypass, please.'

It never failed to send a thrill through his spine. One minute his fingers were holding an inert lifeless piece of flesh, his needle flashing in and out as he sewed it in place, and then, on his command, that empty pouch pulsed into life, bringing hope and a future to a sick child. Sometimes he lingered a moment for no better reason than to savour the miracle before he hid it from the eyes of the curious world. And when the parents plied him with their gratitude he always told them outright: it wasn't *his* gift; he was simply the technician. It was the donor who made the sacrifice; their selfless families who gave the gift.

When he told Rosa Churchill that she burst into tears.

Chapter 23

Carole

'OLIVER CALLED YESTERDAY. *He was in the area. He says it's his only chance to talk about you with people who knew you well. I'm afraid I find it hard to confide anything personal, he still seems like a stranger, but I do make him welcome, Ellie, honestly I do. For your sake.*

'*He seems very smitten with Sarah – you know, the nurse who looked after us through all the donation stuff. Made a big impression, by the looks of it. But she is good – you'd like her – immensely practical and organised, but so kind and understanding. I wouldn't want her job for all the tea in China.*

'*But it's nice that she stays in touch. She's just written again.*

'*Blah blah blah – the usual stuff, thanking us, etc. But then she says:*

> I am enclosing a letter from the man who received Elvira's heart and lungs. Desmond is the father of four children, and thanks to your courage and Elvira's gift, he can now be an active part of their lives and see them growing up.
>
> He has sent us photographs, but we've retained these in our files meantime. We are happy to forward them should you wish, but you need to

think about whether or not you're ready to see
actual pictures of the recipient.'

'I can't decide. Your heart, such an essential part of you.
I'm glad those children have their dad back, though. You'd
have wanted to save their daddy for Willow and Maddie,
wouldn't you, honey, if Drew could have been saved that way?
But then, if he'd lived, none of this would have happened.

'Strange to think, now, all the "what ifs", isn't it? If
Sally hadn't died … if Oliver hadn't been around … if Sarah
hadn't been so honest … if the chaplain hadn't said what he
said … if I'd said no … those children in the letter might be
growing up fatherless. I can be pleased for them, but I don't
want to get sucked into their lives. I thought I might want to
know every last detail, but now it's happened, I don't feel it's
you. I accept that you've gone.

'I hope he looks after your heart, though. I wonder if
they'd tell us if he died. and how I would feel. He's got a big
responsibility, to you as well as his children, specially as your
heart was in tip-top condition. I was reading on the net the
other day, sometimes they use organs from elderly or ill
patients as a last resort if somebody's really, really at the end
of the road, and they can't wait any longer for a healthy young
person to die. But apparently they're obliged to tell the
potential recipient: the donor was a smoker, or had recently
had tattoos, or had hepatitis, or whatever. Imagine! Although
Sarah says when they're that ill most folk don't really care.

'Anyway this man, Desmond, got your perfect young
heart. Lucky him. I'm glad he's an average, ordinary chap, not
some high-powered foreign diplomat, or a wealthy society girl.
You'd have so hated to be part of a privileged world, wouldn't
you? You and your principles!

'OK, shall I read you what Desmond says? Funny
scratchy kind of writing, this one. Not the brightest of the
bright, I'd say.

Hi

I'm no writer at the best of times and what do you

say to somebody that saves your life?

Except thank you.

7 years I was real poorly, couldn't walk 3 steps but I was out of puff. On continuous oxygen at the end. Couldn't even play with my kids. And every night I wondered would I wake up next day? Now I can even play footie with my boys. And maybe in a few years I'll still be around to walk my girl up the aisle. If she gets married that is. More into horses than boys our Trish. Never thought I'd see her grow up even.

But now we have a life, me, the missus, the kids. And that's down to you. I'm putting in a couple of photos, before and after, so's you can see we're real folk and that I'm good as new now. Thanks to your girl.

Bye

Desmond

'A bit of me feels jealous, Ellie. He gets to see his children grow up, you don't. But of course it wasn't his fault you died. And it wouldn't make anything right if he died too.

'Oh, while I think of it, you'll be glad to know that the boys phone more often these days – another of the good things that have come about because of you. They always talk about you. It's nice that. Keeps you very much part of the family.

'And I keep forgetting to tell you, Dad's been brilliant with Willow. She prefers him to me. He's content to let her be herself. He doesn't get upset when she does things you wouldn't want her to do; I feel responsible to you all the time. I'd have struggled with her all on my own, I admit that, she's such a handful. Who does that remind you of?

'It's great that they're developing such a strong bond, too. It'll help them when I've gone. I haven't told anybody, *but I've had to increase my medication lately. I think it's taking hold. But don't worry, I'm not afraid.'*

Chapter 24

Elvira's heart and lungs

ANGUS MCLAREN DROVE like a maniac. The clock was always ticking once the organs were retrieved, but this time, thanks to the weather and those unscheduled roadworks, he was cutting things finer than usual. In the end he managed to squirm out of the queue, whipping down the hard shoulder for the last three miles, arriving with twelve minutes to spare.

In his haste he stumbled on the lip of metal as he hurried out of the lift. His fingers clenched hard on the handle of the cooler, the bold letters of *BIOHAZARD* swinging into view and out again. Vivid images of a comedy programme flashed through his mind: a medic tripping over a drunk patient, the donated heart flying into the air, being caught in the cleaner's bucket, sluiced down the pan, fished out of the sea by a retired colonel, taken to the police on the back of a clapped out motorbike, popped in a helicopter, landing in a howling gale on the roof of the hospital, sewn into place as the clock ticked down the last sixty seconds of viability. *And all because the lady loves Milk Tray!* the slogan mocked.

Nausea tasted sour in the back of his throat as Angus righted himself and his precious cargo. His wife was always telling him he should slow down; 'You're going the right way about becoming a donor yourself.'

'More lovely jubbly organs, huh?' he'd grinned. 'Should have been an air ambulance pilot instead of the terra firma variety. Not so much traffic up there. Cleaner, quicker death too.'

He loved the adrenaline rush and he was totally fascinated by the whole subject of transplantation, reading everything he could get his hands on, talking to anybody in the business who had the time to stop.

His confidence took a knock when one young surgeon told him, 'Remember it's not a cure, it's a treatment. Different set of medications, different set of problems. These patients're on anti-rejection drugs for the rest of their lives.' Kind of deflating that.

But then he'd been thrilled to find the guy sitting next to him in the hospital canteen one lunchtime was a research scientist working with animals – single-minded and passionate about his subject. A golden opportunity to ask: Why wasn't there more xenotransplantation? Why not rear loads of genetically modified pigs to save human lives? The researcher was only too happy to flaunt his knowledge of viral transmission, of unknown pathogens with no known anti-rejection treatment or prevention strategy, of different clotting times. He waxed lyrical on exploitation; no way would he recruit severely ill patients to clinical trials when they had no other viable option. Then off he went on a discourse about public distaste – religious, vegetarian, aesthetic even ... Angus was so engrossed his cheese omelette congealed.

Today he was striding back through the foyer when he noticed a middle-aged woman sitting all alone in one corner, distractedly rocking back and forth, her cheeks streaked with tears.

'You OK, Duchess?' he asked. 'Need any help?'

She shook her head, a fresh paroxysm of grief convulsing her.

'Want somewhere quieter to sit, maybe? There's a nice little chapel a few yards along the corridor. Give you a bit more privacy if you want it. No need to pray or anything.'

She hesitated.

'I can take you there if you want.'

It was dim and peaceful inside, smelling of wax polish and lilies, stained glass windows and sweet funereal music adding to the palpable aura. Angus liked to sit in there himself when things were tough.

The earthy sound of the woman blowing her nose with more vigour than decorum made him smile inwardly. He hoped God had a sense of humour.

'Thanks,' she mumbled through her sodden handkerchief. 'You're very kind.'

'No problem. You look like you could use a friendly face.'

'It's just … my boy's getting a transplant today, and it's touch and go. He might never come out of there alive.' A fresh paroxysm of weeping.

Angus cross-examined himself rapidly. Keep it neutral. No need for her to know what he did.

'Ahhh. Now that's what I call something to worry about. So, what's your boy called, then?'

'Desmond.'

'Desmond, huh? That's unusual. He your only one?'

'No. He's my third.'

'And how old would your Desmond be, then?'

'Forty-six next birthday. Please God.'

'So tell me about Desmond then, what kind of things he likes, what family he's got, what he was like as a lad.'

'Desmond? He was the scamp of the family. Always up to something. Putting worms in the girls' pockets. Smuggling himself in the school coach after he'd been banned from going on the trip to Alton Towers. Caught smoking when he was only eleven. My, but his dad skelped him for that! Smoking. He didn't want his laddie killing himself with fags. But our Desmond – you say don't, he'd say do.

'He saw sense when our Debbie came on the scene, mind. Gave it up quick smart. Sensible lass, Debbie. Pretty too. Don't know what she saw in our Des, but there you go, no accounting. He was such a lolloping lump back then. But she smartened him up and no mistake, and she's been a good wife, stuck with him. Not easy when your man's tied to a chair, gasping for breath, and there's four kids skittering about the place. But that's her, practical, no nonsense, just gets on with it.'

'Been ill for a while, has he? Waiting for a transplant.'

'Seven years. It's his lungs, see. Only he's getting a heart as well – a full set they call it. Works best, heart and lungs all together. Then somebody else gets his heart.'

'Double whammy, huh? Now that's what I call cool.'

'Yes, but … well … think about it … they're taking out … his *heart*.' She dissolved.

'Ahhh. Well, it's a biggie and no mistake, but y'know, they're dead clever here. Don't call it a centre of excellence for nothing. Best in the business. Your Desmond's in safe hands. And you know what? I reckon when he comes round, he won't want his ma to look like she doesn't think he's going to make it. He'll want his ma to look like she's just got him back from the edge, and she's dead chuffed. And she's proud of him for giving his heart to help somebody else. Not many as can say that.'

A glimmer of a smile flickered between the tears.

'That's better. See what a soothing place this is? Now, why don't you sit here for a bit and I'll go and get you a nice cup of tea, eh? Perk you up, ready for your boy coming out of theatre all ready for his new life. Milk? Sugar?'

'Milk, no sugar, ta. It *is* nice in here, peaceful. But I can't pray.'

'Well, that's OK, you don't have to. No rules. Open to everybody this room.'

'When my Desmond got real sick, I couldn't pray any more. Feels like you're asking for somebody else to die.'

'Know what you mean, but you're not, y'know. That other person, they were going to die anyway. All you're doing is praying your boy lives, and I guess pretty much every mother on the planet wants that. And him upstairs,' Angus said in a confidential whisper, stabbing his finger upwards, 'he was so keen on *his* boy, he brought him back from the dead, so I guess he understands too.'

Many hours later Angus put his head round the door of the recovery room. It was several minutes before anyone saw him. His eyes scanned the activity, blue figures darting, machines hissing, lights blinking, alarms shrilling.

'Can I help you?'

'Just wondering about that heart and lungs I brought in earlier. OK? Bloke survive the operation?'

'Yep.'

'Thanks. I'll be off then. Like to know the mad dash wasn't wasted. Didn't risk life and limb for nothing.'

'This bit's only the start. No guarantees in our business.'

'I'm a glass half full man, meself.'

'Best not ask again then.'

His pager bleeped before he could reply.

That night Angus went home and lifted his wife Annette off her feet in a bear hug.

'You been drinking?' she enquired suspiciously.

'Not so much as a thimbleful.'

'So, what have you been up to?'

'Can't a chap hug his wife without getting the third degree?'

'Come on, tell all. I haven't been married to you for nigh on thirty years without learning when you've got something on your mind.'

'Well, if you must know, it was something this wee biddy said today. Her son was having major surgery, see – and I'm talking major, major league here. And I was trying to distract her, like, asking her about him, what kind of bloke he was, what he did, if he had kids, and she reckoned it was her daughter-in-law who'd made him what he is today. Smartened him up, stuck with him, nursed him through his illness, looked after the kids singlehandedly. And that got me thinking. You've done that for me – all bar the illness bit. And how many times have I thanked you? Not nearly enough. So, thanks, Netta, thanks a bundle. For everything.'

'Get away with you, you daft lummox,' she said briskly, swatting him playfully around the ear. 'That's just what women do.'

'Even so.'

'How many lives d'you save today then?' she tossed over

her shoulder as she went to put the kettle on.

'Two hearts, three kidneys.'

'Three? Somebody somewhere needing an anatomy lesson?'

'One wasn't viable apparently.'

'Well, I guess you won't be wanting steak and kidney pie tonight then.'

And with that quip the McLarens segued smoothly into their familiar domestic routines, while Elvira Kennedy's heart beat on steadily, and Desmond Ransome breathed easily for the first time in many years.

Chapter 25

Desmond's heart

THE VOICE AT THE other end was scarcely audible. 'Hello?'

'Mrs Connolly?' Morven said softly.

'Yes.'

'Hi, it's me, Morven King, transplant co-ordinator. Sorry to call at this hour, but can you bring Jade in, please? We have a heart.'

'And this time ... it's ... for real?'

'I can't promise, you know that. But we need Jade here, ready, in case. Hopefully this one will be the one for her. '

'We'll be there.'

Morven gripped the phone tighter. 'Would it be possible to speak to Jade, please? Is she up? Is she OK?'

With two members of her team off sick, the load had been heavy this week. Threadbare nights and junk food didn't help.

Morven stood up, stretched, and caught sight of her image in the mirror. Still slim, still well-toned, still no need for dyes to maintain her natural auburn. She turned slowly to one side. Yes, she was eerily like her mother in appearance and begrudgingly grateful for that. As her dad used to say: 'You're a lucky kid, Morven Gwen. You won't get a finer profile this side of Audrey Hepburn.'

Ignoring the warning voice in her mother's accent – *Stay away from drugs, tobacco and coffee if you want to preserve that skin* – she took a long gulp of her extra-strong brew.

Well, her mother hadn't *needed* caffeine. She hadn't ever dabbled in other people's tragedies, at least nothing more serious than a fashion faux pas or a celebrity scandal. Her daughter's choice of a career made her shudder. 'Please don't elaborate, darling. It's so *animal*.'

Morven thrust the memories away and refocused on the notes in front of her.

Jade Connolly.

They drummed it into you: don't get emotionally involved, but sometimes ... well, certain people just crept under your skin and lodged there. Jade was one of them.

Calling them was the good bit: 'We have a heart.'

After all the anxious waiting, watching life sliding away, not daring to hope, their reactions could be anything from an incoherent scream to a list of reasons why they couldn't simply drop everything right now this minute. In Jade's case it was a long silence ... then, 'Thanks. It's only ... well, I'm sad for that family.'

Special kid, Jade. Totally healthy until she was fifteen, athletics trophy on the mantlepiece, captain of the school netball team, always in the top three academically, able to fashion a bosom friend out of a single sleepover. Gleaming black bob, legs to die for, melting smile. Then wham!

It all started with a common cold that left her unusually tired. Then one night she couldn't breathe properly, her chest hurt. The GP sent her to hospital 'just for reassurance'. Even now Mrs Connolly could hardly bear to talk about the shock of discovery, the heart was more than twice the size it should have been. But Jade trotted out the diagnosis like a pro: idiopathic cardiomyopathy. 'I like it that I'm a mystery to them,' she smirked. She'd arrested twice, and she knew, her parents knew, her brothers knew, the pacemaker would only grant her a temporary stay of execution.

Now, here was a new life within snatching distance and her first thought? For the donor's family.

Her mother was breathless too, rabbiting on, fluttering around Jade, rearranging things. Anything to stop her mind dwelling on the possibility of her only daughter not coming out of that theatre alive. She wasn't ready; she'd never be ready for that.

Jade looked so fragile all gowned up for theatre, woozy with the pre-med, doing her best to smile for her visitor. Morven took the skinny hand in hers.

'Jade, honey, I'm afraid I've got some bad news. I'm so sorry but … that heart? It didn't have your name on it, I'm afraid. I am so, so sorry.'

The grey eyes struggled to focus against the drag of the drugs. 'OK. I understand.' The long eyelashes drooped, stayed shut.

'This one wasn't good enough to use. They can't know for sure until they take it out. And it needs to be perfect.'

Morven saw a solitary tear squeeze past the defences, and let her thumb caress the hand she clasped in both hers.

'I guess I'll still be able to wear that black T-shirt with the scoop neckline, huh?'

Jade's parents were the ones who'd asked Morven to break the news to their daughter. They couldn't. They'd been warned this could happen but it still took the floor from under their feet. To have that cup of hope held to their lips, smell the nectar, and then to have it dashed aside before they could taste it – too cruel.

'Why? Why raise her hopes?' Mr Connolly's words were like hailstones battering against a tin roof.

It brought the reality so close you could smell the blood, and nobody wanted to think too much about the body around that heart, least of all parents of a dying child, but he'd asked the question.

Morven explained all over again. Only she didn't tell them that the man whose heart the surgeons had rejected, was still alive thanks to the healthy organs of an unknown young woman in Scotland. The years of struggling to oxygenate his own damaged lungs had been too much for the heart he was born with.

The consequences hung in the room just above eye-level.

The Connolly family would have to go through this whole thing again, the emotional rollercoaster, the cancelling and rearranging. Or there would be no next time.

She gave them space and a tray of tea and biscuits. Chocolate wafers; Jade's favourites.

It hurt her too, knowing this special kid might be going home to die. Maybe this was a Lorne-moment.

Lorne Blackie.

The notes were dog-eared from being pulled in and out of the filing cabinet. Another special kid. Inspirational. Same wacky sense of humour.

Morven slapped a bright yellow post-it on the front of the folder and wrote 'PHONE LORNE' on it, in red – the colour of emergency.

Lorne was eighteen now and to look at her you'd never know how ill she'd been. Curvaceous figure, beautiful skin, thick blonde curls, full of energy. But under her studiedly fashionable clothes, scars that told a different story, scars that she now wore with pride.

She was thirteen – 'plus two days' she always added with a grin – when the diagnosis stopped her childhood in its tracks. Non-Hodgkins lymphoma.

'It's a busybody type of cancer,' she'd tell other young patients. 'Pokes its nose into blood, bone, lymph nodes. Like a vampire, eh? Hey, have you read *Twilight* and all that series? Stephanie Meyer? Now's your chance. Beats geometry and geography any day!'

But left behind in the hospital after her family had gone home to throw things and bargain with God, Lorne had wept under her pillow, sure she wouldn't see her sixteenth birthday, get her driver's licence, ever be kissed.

The chemo was horrendous. Completely bald, ulcers from her mouth down, unable to eat anything beyond a puree, emaciated and feverish, she spent three months on a teenage oncology ward learning the hard way that bad things happen to good people. The day she walked out she told her consultant, 'You'd better be around when I need a godfather for my first kiddie. You're top of my list.'

Her parents both went part-time, taking it in turns to drive her back to the hospital for another session every three weeks, nurse her in between, protect her from all the dangers lurking in wait for her low immunity. The day they told her officially the treatment was finished, she looked her consultant straight in the eye and said, 'Don't forget, I'm relying on you at the christening.' Defiance, reliance. You'd better be right, chum.

Four months she had of winkling her way back into the carefree teenage world. Then she got up one morning, struggling for breath, unable to stand unaided. Her parents panicked; she was in hospital within the hour. No, they said, no evidence of the lymphoma returning. But ... How cruel was this? Survive the cancer, end up with a heart damaged beyond repair by the chemotherapy.

Days they gave her, at most. She slid in and out of consciousness only vaguely aware of pale faces, stabbing needles, muted voices. The doctor who was misguided enough to suggest it was 'probably best just to let her slip away comfortably', wouldn't ever repeat that mistake! Next thing Lorne was on a machine to help pump blood round her body, and on the waiting list for a new heart. 'How cool is that? Bionic woman, eat your heart out!'

When she regained consciousness properly they asked her opinion. 'We can't guarantee anything though, Mum and Dad count too.'

'Give me the facts then. Real ones, mind. No flannel.'

They spelled it out. 'About a hundred and fifty teenagers have had heart transplants; well over a hundred of them are still alive. Ninety percent of them survive the first year. About seventy percent will need a new heart after ten years; thirty percent in twenty years. The biggest problem is getting teenagers to keep taking the drugs. You'll need them for the rest of your life, no reprieve for good behaviour. If you're meticulous about taking your medication, your chances are better.'

'Where do I sign; where do I go?'

'There are only two centres for transplants for under-sixteens – Newcastle and Great Ormond Street in London.'

'OK. Do I get to fly?'

'Is that a yes?'

'Yeah, man. It's a no brainer. My oncologist'd be dead disappointed if I don't make him a godfather. Things to do before that. Babies don't grow on trees, y'know.'

Her grandmother told her about the day when the world heard about the first heart transplant. 1967 it was. She'd just been into town and bought her first pair of killer heels, red ones. Nobody could believe it was possible. She didn't even know they had proper hospitals in South Africa until then, and now here was her own granddaughter ... Whatever next!

Four weeks and five days later a suitable heart beat inside that indomitable chest. Three weeks after that Lorne Blackie went home. And here she was still planning that christening – once she'd got a degree in history, travelled the world, found Mr Right. Still grabbing the time to talk to other teenagers who quailed at the thought of surgery of this magnitude.

Morven sighed and punched the number carefully, checking it before she let it ring.

'Hi Lorne? How're you doing? ... Busy? Only I have a girl here who could do with your shoulder to cry on and a big dose of your special medicine.'

Chapter 26

Carole

'OH ELLIE, *I very nearly didn't come today. I'll tell you why in a minute. But see, I've brought you a homemade posy. Willow and I made it together. Ivy, ornamental grasses, pansies, daisies, oh, and some fuchsias. Dad didn't turn a hair. Imagine what he'd have said if* you'd *hacked into his precious shrubs when you were her age! It's no florist's dream, I know, but Willow has very definite ideas.*

'*There we are, just for you.*

'*The ballet was good yesterday. Remember, I was taking Willow for the first time since the accident?* Coppélia. *I wondered about inviting her pal Jessie and her mum, but decided it'd be best to try the two of us on our own first, then if it was too much for her, we could come away again. But she stayed for the whole thing and I think she enjoyed it. The costumes were gorgeous, and the scene where the toymaker is inventing things was really funny. Brilliant effects. Willow laughed … it was so good to see her forgetting her injuries and getting lost in the dancing.*

'*Oh, Ellie, seeing her there in her wheelchair, it's so so sad. What wouldn't she give to be up there on that stage dancing her little heart out. Give her her due, though, she rarely mentions her leg. But you do wonder what's going on inside, all the stuff she keeps to herself. Losing both parents, and her sister, and her home, and her leg. Poor lamb, she's had more than her fair share.*

'*I think it'll help when she gets her new prosthesis and*

can move about more normally on her own. But the stump's still giving problems.

'Hey ho. I'd better not start getting maudlin myself. Two things to tell you about today. Two letters actually.

'First, there's another one from Sarah. Not a long one. She says,

Your daughter's liver went to a young adult male who is doing well.

'No details. Makes you wonder. Strange though, we haven't heard anything about Maddie's liver either.

'Anyway, she says this man's doing well, but would they tell you if things went pear-shaped? It is the liver *after all. Was he an alcoholic, maybe? Has he reverted? That really would make me mad – wasting your liver that could have gone to somebody who'd take proper care of it. More than one even because they can split livers, apparently. Probably best I don't know if it was something that could have been avoided.*

'Nothing from the patient himself. That's suspicious too. But then, so many people don't bother with thank you letters nowadays. Would your brothers write in these circumstances? I'm not sure they would. Men are funny about things. You would, I know that, but the boys?

'So many people told us about the letters and cards you sent when they were having a hard time. Bless you for that, Ellie. That was one of the things Oliver loved about you, too, you cared, you were so kind to people. I'm glad he stays in touch. You'd have been pleased about that. Willow keeps up her hate campaign against him, I'm afraid, won't even say his name. If we do she claps her hands over her ears. But your dad and I like him. He only pops in occasionally for a short visit, usually when she's at school. I suspect he's ... but you won't want to know that.

'There, that's the weeds out. Looking neat and tidy. I needed a good old dig today. Although, I can hear you saying, "For goodness' sake, Mum, get a life! I never was into neat and tidy. I'm happy to let things grow over naturally." No, I admit it, this is for me.

'I can't stay long today. Willow finishes early and we're going to make Eton Mess tonight. New recipe, cut out of the paper. Basically meringue, strawberries and cream. I've left the meringues in the bottom of the Aga drying out. But she's going to make the strawberry jam bit and assemble it. You know how she loves summer fruits. And I promise I'll be careful with her cooking the jam.

'There's a terrible temptation to wrap her in cotton wool. Our family doesn't have a good track record in keeping girls alive, does it? But I make myself let her take some normal risks.

'Now, before I go, there's something else I have to tell you. Can't keep putting it off. Another letter came ... last week actually. I needed to think about it before I told you. It was from your publisher. Apparently somebody – some reviewer, I think it is – says parts of two of your poems may have been plagiarised. I'm sure you'd have some logical explanation for this, but of course, we can't defend you. What do we know about poetry?

'Anyway, Dad and I talked about it and we've decided the best thing is just to say, don't publish. We certainly couldn't cope with a big inquiry. We don't want hurtful things being said or even implied, or old scores being raked up. So that's it. The book won't come out now. I'm so, so sorry, Ellie. I know it represents years of work on your part, but your reputation is worth more ... and Willow's memories of you. We'll keep the draft manuscript anyway, and when she's older she can read it and see what a talented mum she had. We know you wouldn't have done anything underhand or illegal in a million years, but it's simply not worth risking everything for the sake of a book.

'Sorry to bring you rather negative news today, honey, but I promised I'd keep you up to date. And it's all taken care of, no need to worry. We won't let anyone discredit you.

'Now I must rush. Willow does not take kindly to me being late. As you know!'

Chapter 27

Elvira's liver

KIMBERLEY SCREWED UP the twelfth piece of paper and threw it forcibly into the wastepaper basket.

'I can't do it. I can't,' she wailed. She clutched her hand to her abdomen as the baby kicked out hard. And again. 'OK, OK, I know I have to, but what on earth d'you say? I haven't even met you yet, but already I love you to bits. Imagine this was you in twenty, thirty years time, my beautiful, talented, gorgeous daughter, killed. Dead. Spare parts going to strangers. What would I want to hear? Me, your Mum. I wouldn't want to even *think* about you all chopped up.' She pulled another piece of paper towards her. 'But I'd take a dim view of the folk on the receiving end if they didn't even bother to say thank you.'

My name is Kimberley, and I used to be a secretary to a firm of lawyers. I wrote umpteen letters a day, but this one – this is something else. It's the hardest thing I've ever had to write.

I'm so afraid of making your pain worse. Please forgive me if I do. I can't even let myself imagine what you're going through. I only want to say an enormous thank you for what you've done for us.

Because of you my Andy has a future, I have my loving partner back, and our unborn child will have a father.

Andy was always healthy and active. He's a lovely, lovely man, and I guess you'll want to know he wasn't a drinker. He only had an occasional beer down the pub with his mates on a Friday, maybe a bottle of wine with me on a Sunday with our dinner.

It was a huge shock when he was taken ill. A virus they think, only nobody could say for sure. Anyway, he just got worse and worse. They tried different things, drugs and everything, but nothing worked. He was on the critical list within days. They told me to expect the worst.

Kimberley stopped and re-read what she'd written. No, you couldn't talk about 'the worst' when that's precisely what had happened to their daughter. She scored through the last sentence.

They said he was facing certain death; only one thing could save him: a transplant.

She closed her eyes against the memories.

Andy, yellow, confused, unsteady, the terrible fatigue, the struggle to get him to drink.

Andy losing his grip on reality, talking rubbish.

The pity in the nurses' eyes, the gravity in the doctor's voice. The grief all around them as the family watched him deteriorate.

The rush to donate – siblings, parents, cousins. The horror as one after the other was rejected … 'incompatible', 'unsuitable', 'sorry, no'.

Andy lapsing into unconsciousness ... 'he may be too ill to survive an operation' … 'there are risks associated with all surgery'... 'he's still very vulnerable. Infection is a real concern.'

The appalled silence of his parents. His oldest sister

weeping: 'I want him to have a tomorrow.' Didn't they all.

Waiting, wondering, fearing he might never come out of the operating theatre.

The nightmare prospect of bringing up their child alone.

How thrilled Andy had been when she'd told him she was pregnant. They'd only been trying a few weeks.

'You been sneaking fertiliser out of the greenhouse?' he'd teased her.

'Must be all that organic stuff you insist on,' she'd retorted.

He'd instantly become all protective, and he'd gone straight out and bought the most enormous teddy bear, reckoned his kiddie should know from the outset he was 'its number one fan'.

'*It?*' she'd protested. 'Babies aren't *its*.' And that's why they'd asked to know the gender. 'Blob' and 'sh-he' became 'she' and eventually 'Kelly'.

They'd planned it all, ever since they'd met, two students far from home, sharing their love of rock music, Turkish food and Russian history.

'We were meant to be,' he'd told her after five weeks. So, how could this be happening? To Andy, who'd prided himself on his low cholesterol, his cold showers, his vegetarian diet, who'd never had a day off work in his life. After all the care they'd taken to be in tiptop condition for conceiving, too.

'I want this kid to be hundred percent perfect,' he'd said, cutting out caffeine and alcohol, overdosing on fresh fruit and veg, bringing home expensive full-price fish and meat.

Your daughter definitely saved his life. No question. I hope that's a wee bit of comfort for you – although I can't imagine how ghastly it is for you hearing somebody else survived and your lovely daughter didn't.

I'm so, so sorry. Really I am. And Andy feels the same. He's cried and cried – we both have –

thinking about her. At first he felt so bad about it
that he didn't recover as he should have. He was
just so wretched feeling he shouldn't have got
her liver.

She shuddered now remembering the weeks after the
operation when Andy'd hovered between life and death. The
terrible sinking feeling as she approached the ICU wondering if
today would be the day. Four weeks he'd battled, touch and
go, then another five weeks in high dependency.

And even when he did turn the corner and head for life,
there were the endless discussions and explanations to help
him overcome his abhorrence.

He was ill for months after his transplant and I
didn't think I should make contact in case the end
of the story didn't turn out right. So, sorry it's
taken me so long to send this. I hope you weren't
thinking we were ungrateful so-and-sos.

They probably were but hey ho, at least now she could
reassure them.

But the painful pictures were still vivid.

Andy so fragile when he was eventually allowed home,
in time for her birthday, every mile taking them further out of
the reach of those who knew what to do, how to recognise
trouble. The terrible burden of responsibility. What if … it'd
be her fault.

Andy shuffling through the front door, skin and bone,
but even so the best present she could ever hope for.

It's very early days yet and Andy has a lot of
catching up to do. He isn't running marathons or
winning medals or anything, but I can tell you he
is appreciating life in a new way now – sunsets,
bird song, lovely music, autumn colours, a picnic,
the baby moving. He says it's like everything's in
glorious technicolour. And it's all thanks to your
daughter – and you.

Would it be too hard for them to hear that?

Both of us feel we have a special bond with your family. We can't ever repay you, but we want you to know that we really, really admire your bravery, and thank your daughter every single day for her special gift. She gave us a future.

I hope it's all right with you, but I pop into church every week and light a candle for her. When Andy's strong enough we're going to plant a tree in our garden in her memory.

And if I knew her name I'd like to call my own baby after her. She's due in two months time. But I quite understand you might not want to write back. It's quite OK. You've done so much already, and in any case I guess her name is probably kind of sacred to you, you might not want a stranger to use it like that.

Andy sends his love and gratitude. He's still pretty emotional about all of this and isn't up to writing himself yet. I hope you understand. It's because he feels too much for you, not because he isn't grateful.

She'd probably tear it up and start again tomorrow but at least she'd made a proper stab at it this time.

Kimberley glanced up and saw Andy moving gingerly down the garden path. Her heart lurched. This new Andy was nothing like the old bouncing ball of energy she'd fallen in love with five years ago. No, the shock of his near encounter with death, coupled with his paranoid dread of harming this precious liver, had certainly taken its toll.

She grabbed her cardigan and followed him to the seat under the old apple tree.

'Your daughter's going crazy, so I thought I'd bring her outside to say, Hi.'

Andy's face broke into its old twisted smile. He laid a hand on her abdomen. 'Oi, you in there, give your mother a break. She's not a drum kit, y'know.'

'Maybe she's playing rugby. You'd better start training yourself or she'll leave you standing.'

He took his hand away abruptly and she saw the shadow fall.

'I'm sorry, Andy, I didn't mean ...'

'I know. Just give me time, Kimberley. It's early days. I'd never forgive myself if I did anything to undo all this.'

They sat in silence and the baby remained motionless. Kimberley placed both hands over her tummy. She felt a tear trickle down her cheek and turned away, but not before he'd seen it.

'Hey, what's up?'

'Nothing.'

'Tell me.'

'I ... well ... I miss the old you. All the fun and ... everything.'

'Me too, but we'll get there. They said at the hospital it'd take time to build up my energy and everything, it doesn't happen overnight. But I'm every bit as keen as you to get back to normal.'

She laid her head on his shoulder and whispered, 'I know.'

'And I can promise you this. There's no way my daughter's going to feel sorry for her old man. I'm going to be her hero, or my name's not Andrew Philip Freeman.'

'Until she hits her teens. Then she'll probably look down on us both with pity, however fit and fast you are.'

There was healing in the shared laughter. It was as good a time as any to tell him, but still she was tentative.

'I've written to the family today. Just a draft. D'you think ... could you bear to read it, and tell me what you think?'

Andy reached out to turn her face towards him, and looked deep into her anxious eyes.

'I don't deserve you. I don't deserve this second chance. Course I'll read it. Maybe even add my own bit.'

'Really?'

'We'll see. Depends how eloquent you've been. You always were better at this kind of stuff than me. But I reckon it's about time I stopped being so pathetic. I mean, look what they've done for me. Least I can do is say thank you.'

'If you want to write it all yourself, that's fine,' she said quickly. 'I've only started it because …' She tailed off.

'Because I've been such a wimp and haven't done anything about it. I know.'

'P'raps we could write it together? I mean, we *both* want to thank them, don't we?'

'More than we can ever put into words.'

'I know. I've tried and tried, and whatever I say seems hopelessly inadequate.'

Kimberley brought her letter outside and Andy read it in silence.

Then he took the pen and added

Hi, this is Andy.

The words don't exist that could capture what I want to say to you.

I honestly didn't think I would survive I felt so terrible. And it's only thanks to your daughter that I'm here today. But I can promise you, I'm going to make sure I make the best of every single day she's given me.

I've been a bit of a wimp recently, dead scared things might still go wrong, but that's no way to repay the debt I owe you. From today I'm going to put my back into being the best partner, the best father, the best person I can be.

Like Kimberley says, we'll never forget your daughter or you, ever. And when she's old enough we'll tell our little girl all about you. I've already got loads of my mates to sign up to be donors. And I hope she will too.

I wish with all my heart you didn't have to go through what you're going through. I saw a little bit what it did to my parents thinking they were going to lose me. But I accept now it wasn't my fault your daughter died; it was my good fortune she was generous enough to give her organs to save others.

I'm sorry it's taken me so long to get round to contacting you. I can assure you, you've been in my thoughts constantly since this happened. I still can't believe people can be this courageous and kind. Thank you, thank you, thank you.

He handed the page to her without a word.

'That's beautiful,' she whispered. 'We'll copy it into a card this afternoon and get it in the post today.'

She gasped. The baby seemed to be turning somersaults.

Chapter 28

Elvira's right kidney

FINN LINCOLN. The transplant coordinator's heart sank just looking at the name.

What a life. In a mere twelve years the lad had been rejected by his father, neglected by his mother, before the children's panel twice for petty theft, absconded from his foster home, sent an old lady into a terminal coma after she found him sleeping in her shed, developed kidney failure, and just risen to the top of the list for a new organ. His deterioration had shocked the medical team who'd retained a healthy scepticism about the truth of some of his symptoms.

But a young mother in her thirties, killed in an accident on Finn's birthday, knew nothing of his history. Her kidney was his for the taking.

Time for young Finn to get to the hospital.

When the phone rang Finn himself answered. He listened in silence, but he wasn't about to conform to the norm any time soon. He had his own conditions: both his parents had to know.

Finn's mother was scathing. 'You'll be on a hiding to nothing telling that waste of space, sure you will,' she'd snorted. 'He'll not be remotely interested.'

But Morven had no option, she had to let Mr Lincoln know. Finn insisted.

Morven rang the number Finn had given her. It went straight

to voicemail.

Seven minutes later her phone buzzed. The Irish accent was broad, the voice coarse and accusing.

'Liam Lincoln. Ye rang me a few minutes ago.'

'Ah yes. Hello. My name's Morven King and I'm a transplant co-ordinator.'

'A what?'

'I help to arrange organ transplants for patients who need them.'

'Well, look, I have no idea why y're ringing me but this here is my mobile. It costs an arm and a leg phoning, so ye'd best get on with it.'

'Of course. I'll ring you back.' It gave her time to open Finn's file, rapidly rehearse what she'd say.

Liam was incredulous. 'Y're telling me he's to be chopped open and get some foreigner's kidney put in'm? Says who? It'll be that spiteful witch that calls herself his mother, I'll be bound.'

'Mr Lincoln, Finn is really, *really* poorly now. If he doesn't get a kidney in the next few days it'll be too late for him. Finn himself wants to have this transplant. But he's anxious to have your blessing too.'

'Look, Miss, I don't know who the hell y'are, but I do know about the scheming whore that got herself pregnant with the boy to spite me. Was she after telling ye that because o' her lies the boy had to go into foster care? Did she tell ye that, now? Did she tell ye that? Sure she didn't, the foul-mouthed bitch. And did she tell ye I hit her? Aye, sure, too right she will've, the lying two-faced slut.'

Morven held her breath. Even over the phone he was intimidatingly aggressive. She'd been told there was a history of domestic abuse, but the truth of the accusations was neither here nor there right now, there were far more pressing issues at stake.

'And because o' her effing lies I've not even clapped eyes on the lad for three years. It'd be "too unsettling, too upsetting," they reckoned. Bleeding social workers! Falling for the lies every time. Well, let me tell ye, Miss Whoevery'are, ye needn't come crying to me now, no, by all that's holy. If he hadn't have asked for me on his deathbed, they wouldn't even have told me the boy was ill. They'd have let'm die without me even seeing'm.'

'But he *is* dying, Mr Lincoln. He really needs your help.'

'OK. Sure I'll help'm.'

Morven startled. 'You ... will?'

'Aye, sure I will. He's my son, isn't he? I'll give'm *my* kidney. I'll not have'm relying on some stranger. It'll be me that saves'm, but it's on one condition.' His distorted vowels were confusing.

'Which is?'

'They give me the boy, let me raise'm. Take'm away from that hell-hole she calls a home. I'll give'm everything he needs. Kidney. Whatever. Wouldn't hesitate. But he has to be mine, only mine, or the answer's no. A big fat juicy, NO.'

'It's not within my jurisdiction to grant you that, Mr Lincoln. But it is my job to tell you how ill Finn is. How desperately he needs your help.'

'I'm not some bleeding old car, y'know, only fit for stripping out the spare parts. I'm not yet forty. Plenty o' life in the old dog yet, so don't ye be thinking ye can browbeat me, young woman. My boy gets me as well as a new kidney, or he gets nothing. Ye hear me? There's the deal.'

'I hear what you're saying, Mr Lincoln, and I'll certainly pass on your message to the people who deal with living donations. Immediately. Please keep your phone on, and with you. Someone will be in touch with you in a bit.'

'And ye can tell that scheming whore that bore'm, she'll not get another cent from me until she agrees to me getting the lad.'

Morven let her breath out slowly. What a relief! She could pass this case over to colleagues in the living donor department. And somewhere, some other family would get the call they were waiting for.

Chapter 29

Carole

'I'M BACK, ELLIE.

'My, your rose is looking lovely. Loads of buds coming too. It's going to be a real picture.

'I was at the hospital yesterday, that's why I couldn't come to visit. They're being really kind. The morphine helps a lot but I must confess it does make me a bit woozy. And the travelling makes me really nauseated, so I had to just stay put. Dad went to collect Willow from school. He told her I had a headache, and she was as good as gold, bless her. We haven't told her the truth about me, time enough for that.

'I'm tons better today. Back like the proverbial bad penny to bore you with my endless chatter. I can't tell you how good it is to be able to share things with you, honey. No fear of any backchat now either, eh, not like the old days?

'Right then, today's news. Another letter about the transplants. I was wondering why we hadn't heard about the kidneys but I guess they don't always get feedback from hospitals, especially if the recipient dies.

'Did I tell you I looked stuff up on the net? Well, anyway, I did. Fascinating it was too. I was surprised, although I guess it means more to me now because it's more relevant.

'Did you know they can do three way swaps with live donors? More than three even; a whole chain of folk. A's partner gives a kidney to C, C's partner gives to F, F's partner gives to A, and so on. But then you'd only need a hiccup at *one point for it all to go pear-shaped. Goodness knows how they coordinate all that.*

'Oh, and then there was this high-flying business man, he offered his kidney to his father. Back in 2008 this was. It all went catastrophically wrong and he ended up needing kidney dialysis himself, and then a transplant from his sister. He sued the NHS for something like fourteen million. Don't know whether he got it though.

'Oh, and did you know that they use organs from executed prisoners in China? Makes you cringe, doesn't it? I definitely wouldn't want one of those. What else would you be getting?

'You can make up to fifty thousand for an organ on the black market. Fifty thousand! Imagine! And to think we gave yours away free gratis and for nothing. We've been swindled! Add up all your bits and pieces and we'd be rolling in it.

'Stem cells seem to be the way forward, though. Growing actual replacement kidneys in the lab. And not so very far into the future maybe. A bunch of scientists here in Edinburgh have managed to grow fetal kidneys from amniotic fluid cells. If you can use the patient's own stem cells you're eliminating the risk of rejection which seems to be a major thing. But of course, there are always the doubters who reckon this'll never get out of the lab, or you'll run the risk of introducing rogue cells that could do more harm than good.

'Listen to me! A mine of useless information that's probably not right anyway. Ignore me.

'Back to you.

'You'll be glad to hear that both your kidneys are alive and well. Great, huh? Listen to what Sarah says first.

… your daughter's kidneys went to a young man called Sam … and an older female patient, Ina.

Sam has sent you a poem with an explanation. Ina has written you a card. I have pleasure in enclosing these.

As I've said before, you are under no obligation

to respond to these communications. If however, you choose to do so, I'm happy to act as postman.

'So, first the lady. Ina. She's sent a card – a sympathy one, I think. Religious looking: a cross, sunrays. Inside it says, Thinking of you, and she's added:

Thank you so much for the gift. I can now leave the house, and I'm planning a holiday. I haven't had one for eleven years.

Yours sincerely
Ina

'The surname's tippexed out, presumably by Sarah or one of her team. I must confess, this one doesn't do much for me. This Ina person doesn't even say what the gift was. It's a bit like a letter thanking you for a Christmas or wedding present where they simply put 'present' as if they can't remember and can't be bothered to check what it was. Standard letter for everybody.

'The boy's letter is completely different. Listen to this, Ellie.

Dear amazing people

I can't begin to thank you for the kidney from your daughter. I'm desperately sorry she had to die but you can bet your life I'm going to take enormous care of the bit of her that came my way.

I'd forgotten what it felt like to be normal. I won't go into the biological stuff – seems a tad indelicate! – but it's brill not having to fit everything in around dialysis, being able to eat normal stuff, plan holidays. Can't tell you.

My sister Patty was hell bent on giving me one of her kidneys, but it'd kill me seeing her going through something like that just cos of me. And what if her one kidney went bad like mine? I mean, imagine how I'd feel! Anyway I managed to fob her off and she was away on holiday when things went downhill fast. I rocketed up to the top of the transplant list, 0-60 in ten seconds flat. And that's when your daughter came to my rescue. It was all done and dusted before Patty got back from abroad. And here I am weeing properly and efficiently exactly like everybody else. Sorry, that just slipped out. But I can't tell you how exciting that is.

So thanks hugely, more than I can ever say. I wish I'd known your daughter. I reckon she must have been one cool chick, beautiful on the inside where it counts. I'm glad. I don't mean to imply she wasn't a cracker on the outside too. They don't tell you anything much about the donor only that she was a young mum, and she was on the register, and her family said yes to the donation. Whatever, she was special, and I guess that makes it even harder for you now. I'm sorry.

I don't know if you like poetry, but I'm a bit of a scribbler. Only amateurish stuff but I found it helped when I was feeling lousy and spending hours wired up to a blinking machine. So I thought I'd scribble one for you to let you know how grateful I am. Don't suppose literary folks'd rate it but it's specially for you, and comes with my undying love and thanks,

Sam

PS. You can bin it if it's too painful.

'Imagine that, Ellie. Your kidney keeping a poet alive! You'd like the poetic justice in that. Doesn't he sound great? So young too. Anyway, here goes with his composition.

He's called it: **You'll never know how much you mean to me.**

In the dark of the night when the world was asleep,
    I'd lie flat on my back and imagine my death:
the coffin, the service, the dark grave, long and deep.
    My mother, my father, my siblings, my Aunt Beth,
all dressed up in their black, hearts failing, all weeping,
    cos my name didn't rise to the top of that list
for getting a kidney implanted for keeping.
'   No match', 'Not fit', 'No use', 'Not in time', they'd insist.
For many a long year I lived through my ending,
    dialysis always the focus and fall-back.
No chance of vacation, of running, or spending
    one shred of energy surplus to need. No slack.
Then one day it happened. The call was, 'It's your turn!'
    The transplanting team went right into overdrive.
The surgeons, the nurses, a chopper, I now learn!
    the porter, the gas man – each one came alive.
I'm under in seconds. When I open my eyes
    it's all over and done: I was fine, I could pee,
I could eat, I could drink. No more ifs, no more lies.
    I've just to recover and return to be ME.
And it's all down to you and your girl. What a star!
    She said yes to the need, she gave hope, she gave life
to really sick people, all with death's door ajar.
    I'm sad that she died though, this daughter, this young wife.
As you grieve and you mourn, I will wrap you in care
    and thank you sincerely – you might have said no, too.
But due to your courage, I'm a lad who can dare
    To dream of a girlfriend, a future, a job – whooo!
I pray for you parents, for your comfort and peace,
    knowing your tragedy isn't lost or in vain,
That one day you'll see her, your aching will then cease.
    You'll all be together, whole and happy again.

'Sorry, Ellie, but it makes me weep because he's been through so much for a young man, and yet he's mature enough to think of us, mourn for us. I'm so glad your kidney went to somebody like that. He deserves it.

'Whoops, I don't think I'm supposed to say that. They tell you, it's not for us to judge the worth of someone's life, or their behaviour or anything, and I'm glad it's not. The transplant people make the assessments on the basis of medical need, not personality or virtue; that's a much better way. But you know what I mean.

I shall treasure that poem. And this time, I think I will send a letter – Sarah forwards them – to let him know how much we appreciate what he says, and him going to all this trouble and everything. And I might even tell him about you being a good poet. He doesn't need to know why you weren't published. Your death's enough reason.

'There's been nothing more from the publisher. I guess that's the end of that saga. Maybe next time I'll tell you why we couldn't risk anyone digging around.'

Chapter 30

Elvira's left kidney

PATTY STOOD STOCK STILL absorbing the sights and sounds and smells of Phuket airport. A group of rowdy youths jostled her as they passed, and she tightened her grip on the handle of her brand new standard issue Samsonite case, one finger reaching down to stroke the pewter cat lucky charm attached to it.

'I'm OK, Sam,' she whispered. 'I'll be fine.'

He'd be so proud of her when she got back: his twin, who'd never been outside Europe before, surviving two weeks exploring Thailand. He'd given her the lucky charm 'to keep you safe cos I can't be there'.

It was hard to believe she was here herself, actually living her dream. She took out her camera and took twelve pictures of the airport just to capture the busyness, the oriental faces, the exotic flowers – oh, everything that she wanted to share with her family.

Strange to think of them, still pottering through their humdrum everyday routines in Reading. Her dad, Malcolm Ingram, opening the shop, selling his greetings cards, newspapers, sweets, tobacco, to the citizens of Berkshire he'd served faithfully for over two decades. Her mum, Cynthia, helping the next generation at the local primary school to put expression into their reading (an obsession of hers), and to have the right money when they went into Ingram's shop for sweeties.

Her older brother, Ryan, working all hours to get his

own computer business up and running ready for life after university; in his spare time active in the Green party.

Her twin, Sam ... ah, Sam, all his energy spent on simply hobbling through life, doing his best to struggle to college any day he could, five times a week strapped to that confounded machine, 'Dracula Mark Four', to do the work his polycystic kidneys had given up doing.

She gave herself a shake; no point in getting all emotional. She'd find her hotel, leave her belongings safely locked up, and then start the great adventure in earnest, storing everything up for Sam too. And each day she'd commit the experiences to her laptop, ammunition for several assignments. What an opportunity! She could see it now, an article in the *Sunday Times* or maybe the *Daily Telegraph* travel pages: *Sheffield University journalism student wins top prize for travelblog through Thailand.*

All her mother's fears about tsunamis and earthquakes and pickpockets and organ traffickers and pickpockets and kidnappers could be relegated to history. And Sam would have no more excuses for refusing her kidney.

She'd pestered him, day after day, but he'd remained adamant.

'You've got to have a life first, Pats, see the world. Besides you might have a kid yourself one day, and he might need a kidney, then where would you be?'

'Look, you idiot, chances are nobody else in the family will ever need a kidney. But *you* do, and I'm a match on all six antigens for you. How rare is that? Less than a quarter of the time that happens, so don't look a gift horse in the mouth.'

'You don't need that level of compatibility nowadays, not with the immuno-suppressants they've got today. I don't want *you* taking risks when I can have a kidney from somebody who's died and doesn't need it any more.'

'They wouldn't make it legal for live donors to give a kidney if it was dead risky now, would they? Stands to reason.'

'Still a risk though.'

'But if *strangers* do it, for goodness' sake! I'm not even

being altruistic or noble or anything; I'm being completely selfish. I don't want to lose my twin. Only got one, and I've kind of got used to having him around. Come on, Sammy, talk sense. You'd do the same for me.'

'Maybe. But I'm not desperate yet, and I don't want you taking chances for me till I am.'

'I can have a totally normal life with one kidney, still see the world, paint my bit of it red. And besides, I'll enjoy it all much more if I'm not worrying myself sick about you, you stubborn old moron.'

But he'd been immovable. 'Maybe later' was as much as he'd concede.

'I know what it is! You're too chicken about having a girl's kidney,' she'd taunted him. 'Afraid you'll get my phobia about spiders.'

'Or your passion for gnocchi. Yeuch! Too right I am!'

'Well, why don't we pair up with another family, then? I swap my kidney to their relly; you get one from her brother.'

'Just can it, Patty. Nag, nag, nag. You're doing my head in.'

As the day of her departure approached he pulled his own ace out: 'I might even have a new kidney by the time you get back. *That* would get you off my back.'

'You let me know the second you get word, boyo, or else. You needn't think I'm going to carry on swanning around on holiday while you go through that operation. Promise me now. Promise.'

'OK. Though it'd be a lot more peaceful here without you pestering me all the time. And just you remember, keep your big trap shut out there, Patty. If they find out you're willing to be a donor, they'll whip out your kidney anyway, and give it to somebody else who needs one. And it'll be a butcher not a highly trained surgeon on the other end of *that* knife.'

He'd shown her the website that reported the facts. They flashed through her brain now, loaded with extra significance now she was here in the very country it talked about.

Over 7,000 organs have been sold to foreign nationals, one of the Sunday supplements had reported, *desperate private patients*. Who'd care about an unknown English tourist wandering round Thailand on her own?

There is already a blackmarket in human organs in parts of Asia. Poor people got ... what was it? Up to one thousand five hundred for a kidney? – she couldn't remember what currency they'd used – one thousand five hundred somethings anyway. No, no one would ask questions out here; they'd probably make jokes about transplant tourism. This wasn't the land of human rights.

How Sam had laughed telling her about the man who'd sold his wife's kidney to buy a second-hand tractor without her knowledge. 'Keep it for a rainy day, sis. Who knows when your hubby might need a new tractor.'

Was he laughing still?

His image swam before her eyes, always tired, pasty, no energy, water-logged. Always in and out of hospital, always staring death in the eye. She could hardly remember a time before the kidney failure. Why, oh why did he have to be so stubborn?

He'd crowed when the call came back in January: 'We have a kidney.'

'See, I told you it'd work out.'

She'd prayed that night, harder than she'd ever prayed for anything in her life – 'Keep him safe, God. Don't let him die.' – because you never knew with operations, and after all these years of dialysing, he couldn't be in tip-top condition, that's why he needed the transplant.

It had been like a body-blow hearing the news next morning. She'd dreaded going in to visit him, but he was upbeat.

'Somebody else needed it more, Pats.'

She'd wanted to rage and fight and *do* something. 'Come on, Sam, have mine. You're all ready now. Let's do it and then put this whole thing behind us.'

But he still refused. 'I'm on the list, at the top, kid. It'll be OK next time.'

And now she wasn't even available ...

Her father couldn't disguise the wobble in his voice when she finally got through to him.

'Oh Patty, thank God …

'I'm fine, Dad, I'm fine. Flight was an hour late getting here, and then it took me a while to find the hotel, get myself booked in. Boy, it's hot. Humid too. I'm drenched already and I've only just had a shower.'

'We were trying to get hold of you …'

'Sorry, switched my phone off for the flight, and then in all the excitement I forgot to put it back on again. Sorry.'

'Sam wanted to speak to you himself.'

'Put him on, Dad. I've got so much to tell him already.'

'He's not here, Pats. He's at the hospital.'

'Hosp … Dad, what's happened?'

'He suddenly deteriorated. They say … they say, unless he gets a kidney within the next twenty-four hours …'

'I'll be on the next flight. With his kidney. This time he can't say no.'

'Thanks, love. I'll get back to the hospital now.'

'Dad, tell him to hang on in there. I'm on my way.'

She was twenty-one hours too late.

Elvira Kennedy's kidney was already cleansing Sam's blood by the time Patty burst into the hospital ward and collapsed on the floor beside his bed, having fasted for twelve hours in readiness.

On his bedside locker was an envelope with her name on it. Her hands shook as she turned it over slowly, suddenly fearful of what it contained.

Gotcha, sister.
Life's a twister.
You're still intact,
I've now been hacked.
No more nagging,
No feet dragging.
A brand new part:
A fresh new start.

Yippee!
Only you shouldn't have cut short your holiday.
Get back out there and see the world!

'Your flipping poetry sucks,' she whispered in his ear.

Eight weeks later Sam handed her a letter.
'How about that, huh? Imagine bothering to reply.'
Patty read it twice.

Dear Sam

We were so touched by your lovely letter and especially your poem. Elvira was a poet – she's had a few published – and she'd have been tickled pink to know her kidney was used to keep a fellow poet alive.

It helps to hear that you are doing so well. Keep it up. It's a comfort to the family knowing some happiness came to others through our tragedy.

All the best

(Elvira's parents)

The signature had been scored out.
'Well, what d'you know?' Patty said. 'A poet, huh? What are the chances of that?'
'Just think, if I hadn't started scribbling my stuff till after the transplant, we'd have thought the talent came with the kidney.'
'Talent? What talent?' Patty scoffed. 'Maybe hers will give you more of a chance, though. You can but hope.'
But the letter had sparked another train of thought for Patty. Travels through Thailand might have fallen by the wayside, but another opportunity beckoned.

Chapter 31

Elvira's left kidney (continued)

IT HAD TO BE the same person. Elvira wasn't a common name, and the date of the accident fitted with the date of Sam's transplant. The Scottish newspaper reports gave the full names and ages of Elvira Kennedy, her dead husband, her children and her parents – a head start.

Thank goodness for electronic searches; piecing together the story with so many keywords wasn't difficult, anybody with a bit of computer savvy and a modicum of determination could do it, but if she was to make her mark as a journalist, Patty needed to see what no one else saw, find that spark that sold newspapers – what Professor Blackridge called 'sensation in a sentence'. She'd have to get photos, interviews, verbatim accounts, alongside that intriguing story line.

A trip to Scotland didn't equate to a fortnight in Thailand but it offered the potential for that unusual angle, as well as doing something for Sam. Had to be worth a go.

She soon had the basics: the Beachams had moved to Edinburgh when Elvira was four, from the tiny village of Edderton beside Cambuscurrie Bay way up on the east coast. She jotted down her plan of campaign:

1. visit Edinburgh
2. take sight-seeing coach trip to the Highlands
3. visit the place where Sam's donor lived as a
      toddler.

At the very least she'd get a feel for a childhood lived in this remote part of the country, and a few atmospheric pictures to illustrate her text.

The grave provided a good emotive start: the simplicity of the stone, with its stark information; the carefully tended plot; the single white rose. But it felt wrong. Why was Elvira alone? Where was her husband? Why no references to those she loved, and who loved her?

The husband's grave was six rows away. No flowers on this one, and much more significantly, no other coffins in beside Drew Frederick Kennedy, even though it clearly stated 'beloved husband of Elvira' and 'adored father of Willow and Madeline'. So why … ? A family dispute, maybe?

Curiouser and curiouser. Patty's imagination went into overdrive.

The tour through the Highlands was far more beautiful than she'd expected but too rushed for her artistic soul. The chatter of her fellow travellers broke her concentration, and she struggled to stay abreast of the place names and capture the scenes she wanted to share with Sam.

By contrast, alone in the tranquillity of Edderton, she had time to think and plan.

The actual house the Beachams had sold so unexpectedly (so the neighbour, Mrs Hattie Campbell, said) was unexceptional: stone built, dormer windows, solid front door, all typical of the Highlands. Patty had photos in the camera before Mrs Campbell came out to see if she could help.

'Can you tell me anything about them as a family?' Patty asked with her most beguiling smile. 'I'm assembling a record for someone close to them and any stories that bring the family to life would be invaluable.'

'A nice couple, the Beachams. Quiet, mind, kept themselves to themselves for the most part. They weren't from round here, see. He worked in business of some kind. Away a lot. She was more of a home-bird, doted on her bairns. Four she had: two boys, then two girls. But when the wee one died – you know about that, I daresay?' Mrs Campbell said, her soft accent caressing the child.

'Sally, the youngest, you mean?'

'Aye.'

'I know she died at a few months old.'

'Aye.' Mrs Campbell gave her a sharp look. 'But best be careful what you say on that one. We reckoned there was more to it than they let on.'

'Oh?'

'Aye. Well, they *said* it was a cot death, only … well, have you talked to Libby Nairn at number 15?'

'Not yet, no.'

'Well, she was the social worker around here at the time. It's ages ago, mind, all of thirty years, I shouldn't wonder, but one day she let slip it wasn't what they made it out to be. You'd best talk to her.' Mrs Campbell glanced at the clock on her wall. 'She'll like as not be home right now. She always makes sure she's in for *Countdown*.'

Mrs Libby Nairn was indeed in, and happy to see a fresh face in her remote village. She looked about seventy but her step was sprightly and her eyes remained inquisitive.

'This is such a beautiful place to live,' Patty began, gesturing to the surrounding countryside.

'Aye, it is,' Mrs Nairn said, her voice lilting over the syllables. 'Specially on a day like today. But you'd not be so keen to linger when the snell wind blows in from the east, I can tell you.'

'I can imagine,' Patty smiled.

'So what brings you to my door?'

'You'll remember Elvira Beacham, I guess, given what happened?' Patty began.

'Wee Elvira. I do indeed. How could I forget?'

'And I guess you've heard that she died not long ago, killed in a car crash? Her and her little girl, Madeline.'

'Word did reach us.'

'A real tragedy.'

'Aye. But … it was really an accident? They're sure this time?'

'I believe so,' Patty said hesitantly. 'At least all the reports say it was.'

'Well, I hope so. I wouldn't want any more deaths on my conscience.'

'Mrs Nairn, I know there were all sorts of rumours about Sally's death, but I'm keen to put the record straight. Seems like other people suffered because of what happened. Mrs Campbell said you were the best person to tell it like it really was.'

'You're not from the papers, are you?'

'Oh no. Just interested,' Patty said. 'Someone close to me is connected to the family.'

'Well then, I see why you'd want to know.'

'Elvira was only a tot herself, wasn't she?'

'Well, she was, but my word, the devil was in that lassie and no mistake. She wasn't your average wee bairn.'

'Ahh.'

'Of course, the law says kiddies of that age can't be expected to know right from wrong, but in my book that lassie knew exactly what she was doing when she killed her sister. I said as much at the hearings and everything. I always feared she'd go on to do far worse, but they wouldn't listen. Reckoned it was simple sibling jealousy. *They* didn't see her in one of her rages.'

'So what do *you* think happened?'

'Well now, my lips are sealed on that. I can't give chapter and verse, even yet, though it weighs heavy on my conscience. The whole thing was held behind closed doors. But there isn't a day goes by but I don't wonder: if I'd spoken up early on, would wee Sally be alive today?' She sighed deeply. 'But, I kept schtum, gave the lassie the benefit of the doubt, and look what happened.'

Patty waited, hardly daring to breathe, but when nothing more was forthcoming she ventured a prompt. 'So they moved away, had a fresh start, putting the past behind them.'

'That's the theory. But yon lassie took that evil temper with her.'

Patty nodded, holding her breath.

'It was a relief, though, I can tell you, when they moved out of my patch, not my responsibility any more. I always wondered what would become of her, but she vanished off the system soon after they moved. Guess that's what they do to protect these children. Me, I reckon we need to protect other people's bairns. But I've said enough, more than I should have, maybe. Elvira's dead now, God rest her soul. She'll not be harming anybody ever again.'

Patty murmured something sympathetic but her mind was racing.

She spent a further hour in the local pub, wandered through the village, dangled a few carrots, but thirty-two years is a long time, and most people had moved away or died since the Beachams had lived here, and no one else was prepared to divulge anything they might or might not have been told. She had to accept that it was only the social worker's conscience that had led her anywhere, and content herself with photographs: *Edderton as it is today*.

Sam read the first draft of Patty's assignment without uttering a word, before lifting his head to stare at her open-mouthed. 'She was a ... *murderer*!'

'She was only four years old,' Patty said, taken aback by the effect of the revelation on her brother. 'She must have changed. She had kids of her own, she donated her organs to people.'

'Even so ... I've got part of a killer inside me?'

'Well, I *told* you you should have had mine.' She tried to inject humour into the words. 'You've no one to blame but yourself.'

'What did she do? How did she do it?'

'I don't know, I couldn't find out anything else. I didn't dare raise Mrs Nairn's suspicions by probing for any more. And it all went underground after the family moved away. But, Sam, it doesn't matter ... to you, I mean, does it?'

'Not matter?' he hissed. 'Of course it *matters!*'

'But why?'

'They said she was lovely and a poet and generous and kind – these people that know I've got her kidney. But she wasn't. She was a devil, the social worker says so. And a murderer. And she's in me.'

'No, only her kidney's in you.'

'Well, I don't want *any* of her in me. I'll have to get it taken out.'

'Sam, you can't! They wouldn't do that anyway, not another operation that you don't need.'

'I *do* need it.'

'Not from a medical point of view you don't. You certainly don't. Don't be daft. And it would probably kill you, another operation, going back on dialysis, and everything. '

'For once in my life I wish I'd listened to you. Somebody else would be alive now with her kidney, not knowing anything bad about her, and I'd have yours, and none of this would have happened.'

They were both silent, taking in the significance of what they now knew, before Patty spoke, her words slow and heavy.

'If you hadn't written to those parents; if they hadn't written back to you; if I hadn't been trying to impress the Prof, we wouldn't have ever known.'

'I'll need to write to those parents again.'

'No, Sam! You can't! You *mustn't*. It'd destroy them. They must be so sad and hurting. You know that, you said that last time. Besides, Sarah wouldn't pass it on; she couldn't. And we'd all be in trouble for letting information out and following things up we shouldn't have.'

'We don't need to go through Sarah. You know where they live.'

'But I'm not saying, I'm absolutely not, Sam, so don't bother even *trying* to wheedle it out of me. I already wish I'd never started this whole wretched thing. Damn getting a good mark for my assignment, it was never worth this. There's a very good reason why they keep all this stuff anonymous.'

After she'd gone, Sam sat staring at the computer screen for an age before he began to tap out his message.

Dear Mr and Mrs Beacham

I'm writing to let you know that I've now found out

about your daughter's past – why you left
Edderton, why she's buried alone. And I feel sick
– about the lies and the kidney and everything.

I can't bear the thought that I've got something of
her inside me, and I'm going to see if they'll take
it out again.

I just wanted you to know that that'll be the end
of it. She won't live on through me if I can help it.

He saved it to be edited later when he'd calmed down,
Patty's parting words echoing somewhere in his head: 'You're
not thinking straight, Sam. Just give it some time. You're alive,
aren't you? Fitter than you've been for years. And that's
thanks to Elvira. Remember that. But she's dead, poor
woman ... poor family.'

He'd just finished tracking Guy Beacham down on the
web where he advertised his services as a freelance consultant,
complete with contact details, when Patty popped her head
round the door.

'Just come to tell you, I've been thinking, and this whole
thing feels wrong to me. So I've decided, I'm not going to
submit the full story for my assignment; I'll doctor it.'

'Why?'

'Whatever the rights and wrongs of what happened
thirty-two years ago – and we don't know what did, remember
– that woman saved your life. It'll scupper my chances of
getting top marks, but I'm blowed if I'm going to do anything
to deny that. We owe her.'

'Whatever,' he said.

'*You* owe her, more than anybody. And you might at
least be grateful I tried to find out for you,' Patty said huffily.
'It's not my fault it wasn't what you wanted to hear.'

'Thanks, kiddo. Sorry about your assignment though.'

She flounced off leaving Sam with his finger hovering
over the Print key.

Chapter 32

Carole

'ME AGAIN, ELLIE. Boy, it's cold today. I'm into winter woollies. Or maybe it's me. Not much meat on the old bones these days.

'So what's new? You know about the big things but I haven't filled you in on the other bits and pieces. Tissue, valves and stuff. You don't hear so much about them but they're important too.

'When Sarah was telling us all about donating she said that sometimes they couldn't get all the usual organs. Maybe it was too long after the death for them to use the heart, but they could maybe take the valves. Or maybe the next of kin couldn't agree, so they'd compromise, leave the main organs, take tissue that didn't have the same significance.

'In our case, we said they could have everything just as you wanted, but I'm specially glad they got bone. Sarah's letter says,

> We also took some bone to be used for a
> number of operations to save the limbs of young
> people ...

'I know they can't give Willow a new leg, but it's something if we ... you've been able to help other kiddies walk again.

'I do worry about Willow, Ellie. I know she's had a hard time, but she's so ... resentful. Spiteful sometimes. We try to steer her, honestly we do, but it's hard to deny her things when she's been through so much. Only ... well, who knows where it'll lead?

I scrutinise the cemetery in every direction. Not a soul in sight. Even so I drop my voice. Just in case.

'Your Dad says my fears are groundless, there's a rational explanation for Willow being as she is. She's grieving, trying to make sense of all her losses: Drew, you, Maddie, her home, as well as her leg, but if we're brutally honest, you and I both know she was a disturbed little girl before all this happened. She's your daughter. She's been difficult from the outset, just like you were. Can these things be inherited?

'Dad also says you were too young to understand what you were doing. You weren't inherently evil or cruel or anything, it wasn't anything genetic you could pass on. But of course, you don't know the full story.'

I rush on before I lose my nerve – again. 'I promised I'd tell you. Today's the day.'

I do another scan of the cemetery.

'It goes back to when Sally was born. You were only four, but you were terribly jealous of her. I'd catch you sometimes giving her a pinch, poking her, rocking her fiercely, with such an expression on your face. You told me to send her back, get rid of her. I tried to involve you, let you be a little mother to her, but you weren't interested. You simply didn't like her; you resented her.

'Then one night ... Oh, Ellie, one night I found you in her cot. You'd taken your quilt in with you, climbed in beside her, wrapped her tightly in the quilt and then lain on top of her. The poor little thing ... couldn't breathe. By the time we found you both, it was too late.

'We were devastated, of course. But you were only a tot, well below the age of criminal responsibility. The doctors, the police, they all agreed, no point in ruining your life too, so they hushed it up. We told people it was a cot death, which in a way it was, and that's what we told the boys. People didn't know as much about cot death back then. There was an inquiry of course, had to be, but they kept that low key as well. Social work came, did assessments.

'*And we moved here, where nobody knew us, nobody asked questions. And eventually it faded and we carried on with our lives.*

'*I watched you like a hawk all the time, fearful of how you'd turn out. You were a troubled child, no doubt about it, Ellie. Much as I loved you, I struggled to like you sometimes. You had a cruel streak, and you were so rebellious. And of course, as you grew older you became more sophisticated in the ways you showed that rebellion. The teen years were ... well, you deliberately defied us, me especially – Dad wasn't around most of the time.*

'*But then, after you left home and went to university, things changed. You threw all your energies into studying; you became passionate about helping the underdog, righting society's wrongs.*

'*Then along came Drew, and you blossomed into a different person altogether. He – and later the girls – softened you. Even when Willow turned out to be an almost exact replica of you, you didn't revert. You understood her, you had so much more patience with her than I had with you. It was lovely to watch you. Thank you for giving us those good years, Ellie.*

'*But the accident blew everything wide open again. Suddenly the police were involved, the Inspector found out about Sally and you, and he came to the hospital, told me he knew. He was kind though, reassured me about the press. But I thought, well, if he can put two and two together, so could other people. That's why we buried you here, away from the main paths, not with Drew, just in case. And we only put your married name and dates on your headstone.*

'*Then someone started to lay flowers on your grave. Someone who knew too much about you. When that business with the poems happened, we couldn't risk any kind of investigation in case all this stuff came out. So we pulled the plug on the book straight away, just to be sure. I couldn't bear to have horrible things said about you, speculation, innuendo, anything. I couldn't bear it.*

'*Of course, they can't hurt you now, but they could hurt Willow. I want her to keep only good memories of her mummy. Because you were a good mum, Ellie, you were. You really were.*

'Oliver told me that he was the one who made you late that day, made you speed. It was good of him to admit it; no one would have been any the wiser if he'd simply kept quiet. Poor chap, he's struggling with his conscience, I know. But it's to his credit that he didn't want your name besmirched. You weren't a reckless driver, you were only trying to please your daughter.

'He told me something else too. He meant to go on the donor register, only he's still not got around to doing it. He feels bad about it though, because he told Sarah he would. But I reckon that happens a lot, people having good intentions but not acting on them.

'So there it is, Ellie, I've finally told you. No more secrets. I'm so, so sorry about everything – Sally, you, the hard times, all the years of watching you so closely, worrying, the poems. If I could have changed it, I would have.

'Was it my fault? Did I make you into that tortured child? If so, I'm desperately sorry for that too. But I want you to know, I only did what felt right at the time. I did it all for you. You children were my life. I never ever for one second stopped loving you.

'It's a great relief to have this out in the open at last. Now I can concentrate on being all I can be for Willow while I'm still here. I'm going to go into a hospice towards the end so Willow won't see what happens, and Dad can spend all his time keeping things stable for her. It's a good thing it's him not me who'll be left to bring her up. I know he'll be a good guardian for her, and he'll guide her and support her better than I would. Now he's retired he's got so much more time to be a good parent, and he doesn't have all my baggage. He'll give her the freedom to fly; I'd be forever clipping her wings.'

Chapter 33

Willow

IT'S NOT FAIR.

Ballet was the one thing I wanted more than anything else in the whole world. But now ... This stupid prosthesis is useless. Look at it. Clumsy great thing.

I don't see why they can use bits of Mummy and Maddie to help other people – *strangers!* – but not me. It's just not fair.

At first Granny wouldn't tell me, but I kept asking and asking and asking. She's afraid to get cross with me, so I knew she'd give in in the end. Now I know all about the hearts and the lungs and the liver and kidneys and everything. And the bone.

I asked her, 'If they took out the bones, what did Mummy look like? She'd only be a heap of jelly.'

We did skeletons at school so I know about it.

Granny didn't like me asking, it made her cry. But in the end she asked somebody called Sarah who reckons they put in prostheses pretty much the same as mine, only they sew them in so the legs and arms and everything look like normal. I wish I could've seen it. Weird though, I think. I mean, nobody *sees* the person in the coffin, do they? Why bother?

Makes me feel kind of shivery knowing things from inside Maddie are walking around. And Mummy. Who are these people that're partly them? I look at people in the street sometimes and wonder, is it her? Is it him? Is it her?

But I know it's not me. It'd be nice having Maddie's leg.

All they had to do was make it grow really fast till it was my size. But no. Grandpa says that sort of thing doesn't happen in real life, only in story books, but I'm not a fool. I *know* they do this sort of stuff in labs. I've seen it on Google. They could have, if they'd wanted to.

But it fits. Granny says Mummy was always helping other people, even she didn't know how much. Helping other people, yeah. Only not me.

Chapter 34

Sarah

THE PACKAGE LEFT lying on her desk simply said, *'For Sarah'*. Inside was a simple polished wooden box with a tag attached to the brass clasp. *A collection of assorted positive vibes to cheer you when the going gets tough. Rx*

It was filled with heart-shaped confetti.

She ran her finger lightly over the burnished wood and then held it gently in both hands. The Ruaidhri she was getting to know was constantly surprising her, a far cry from the robust professional shoulder she'd so often leaned on. He was more flirtatious, more tender, more exciting and unpredictable, than she'd expected.

She couldn't quite believe in their new relationship yet, but was all too aware of the continuing need to work with him whatever the outcome. When she'd raised the issue with him he'd stood to attention with a Boy Scout salute.

'I promise to be the soul of discretion and decorum at work, to observe the rules of propriety at all times, to honour God and the Queen.'

But his expression often belied his distance.

She smiled now remembering as she placed the box carefully in the top drawer of her desk, and turned to the pile of letters awaiting her attention.

She worked steadily for a good twenty minutes before a card made her pause. It was from Carole Beacham. Memories flooded back; so much tragedy for one family. And she often wondered what the future held for young Willow.

Dear Sarah

I'm writing to say a very big thank you for everything you did to help our family at a terribly difficult time.

I had huge reservations about donating Ellie's organs initially, as you know, but I can honestly say none now. It has been a real source of comfort to me – and to Guy – to know that some good came out of Ellie's untimely death.

We so much appreciate your staying in touch and forwarding the letters from recipients. It helps to know these people are alive because of her.

Willow seems to be progressing well. She gets around easily on her prosthesis, and seeing the amazing achievements of athletes in the Paralympics has given her a real boost. She's got her eye on a world record!

Just so that you know, I'm in the terminal stage of cancer myself now, so it might be best if you address any further correspondence to Guy.

Bless you for all the wonderful work you do.

Sarah sighed. What a tough life they'd had. Now this. She wrote a reply immediately lest it be too late.

She was turning back to her computer when there was a tap at her door. What now?

Ruaidhri peeped into the room. 'Am I permitted to come any closer?'

'Of course. Come on in. You must be telepathic. I was just about to send you an email.'

'In my safe and reassuring chaplaincy role?'

'Naturally. I'm on duty. In professional mode,' she said primly.

'Pity.' He grimaced.

She shook her head at him. 'I was going to let you know about Carole Beacham. Remember? Mother of Elvira Kennedy. Young mum killed in a car crash? The wee girl died too. You saw them a couple of times when Carole was swithering about donation.'

'I do remember. The girl with the amazing red hair.'

'That's the one. Sad news, I'm afraid. She – Carole, I mean – is now terminally ill herself. Which means the granddad will be left with the other little girl, the one who survived but lost a leg, remember? Life does suck sometimes.'

'It does indeed. Nothing much reassuring to say on this one, but I do sympathise.' He reached across to lay a hand over hers, adding quickly, 'Purely professional.'

'Thanks. You're always such a solid comfort.'

'Can I help? Other than offering distraction after work, I mean.'

'Actually, maybe you can. Tell me what you think. We could only use the heart and liver from the wee girl, Madeline, and they know that. But the liver wasn't a success. Should I tell them? Would you want to know, d'you think? Is that better than being left in the dark about it?'

'Hmm. Tricky one. What d'you usually do?'

'I tell them what we've used, and follow that up with the success stories as we get news.'

'But in this case? You feel that's not enough?'

'I don't know. This one is particularly tragic; the Beachams lost two girls. They know *Elvira's* organs are doing well – heart, lungs, liver, kidneys. They know Madeline's heart was used successfully too, but they must wonder about her liver.'

'I suppose if you say nothing, they can at least hope, can't they? Maybe just think the recipients haven't got back to you yet, or something.'

'That's pretty much my thinking. Thanks.'

He touched her arm briefly. 'Anything else I can do?'

'Not unless you can prepare my lecture on the pros and cons of a system of opting out for next week's conference.'

'No sweat.' Ruaidhri drew himself up straight, adopted a pompous voice and began ticking off items on his fingers.

'One. Presumed consent turns volunteers into conscripts. Rather like plundering old cars for spare parts.

'Two. It relies on inertia and ignorance to get what the government and NHS wants. Our local MSP invented inertia so he'd be OK with that.

'Three. It undermines the trust patients have in their doctor. Is this gorgeous hunk of manhood eyeing me up as a potential organ factory or because I'm hot?

'Four. It's expensive. You'd need pots of money to change the infrastructure, and educate the public and modify society's attitudes, and build in safeguards, and increase resources to handle improved outcomes. And right now this little old country ain't exactly well endowed with legacies and bequests from rich spinster aunties.'

Sarah stared at him open-mouthed. 'I was ... kidding.'

Ruaidhri continued in the same ponderous tone. 'Five. It carries a connotation of pressure, coercion even. Do it because it's expected, not because you believe in altruism. Arm up the back, thumb-screws at the ready. We Britons are proud of our culture of altruism. "Do unto others" and all that jazz.'

'Hold on a minute,' Sarah interrupted. 'How d'you know all this stuff?'

'Thought I might get an extra brownie point or two if I mugged up on the subject and had a passing knowledge of what you do for a living. All part of a longer-term strategy.'

Sarah shook her head, unsure whether this was more of his teasing. 'How on earth d'you do it?'

'Do what?'

'Remember all this stuff. Lists of things.'

'I'm a nerd. A geek. I like facts. My brain's wired to think in terms of mind-maps and tedious things like that.' He paused, looking at her rather sheepishly. 'Actually ... I'm also doing a PhD in this area, looking at the role of the chaplain in relation to decision making in hospitals. The ethics of medicine. Whose body? Whose decision? Whose responsibility? – those sorts of questions. Plus I give the odd lecture at the university. Sorry.'

'Seriously? Or is this more of your nonsense?'

'No, seriously.'

'Well, sounds to me as if *you* should do this lecture instead of me. I'd far rather listen to your chatty style and funny asides than to me boring on.'

'Rubbish. You couldn't make it boring if you tried. You know it inside out and back to front, and you can bring it alive with anecdotes, real life stories that touch people's hearts. Much, much more convincing. Everybody likes a story. You'd have them weeping in sympathy if you told them about Elvira Kennedy. They'd all be rushing to sign the register.'

'So ... are you not really a chaplain?'

'Oh yes, I am – fully paid up, but part time. I'm not an undercover agent or anything sinister, so fear not, your secrets are safe with me. But the rest of the time I'm a post-grad student in the divinity faculty, at New College, hoping eventually to do more lecturing in the practical and pastoral side of theology. I genuinely do find the whole subject of medical ethics fascinating.'

'Wow. I'm impressed. But I don't know why you didn't say anything about this before.'

'Sounds too pretentious.'

'You – pretentious? I don't think so.'

She wished devoutly that Ruaidhri was in her place on the platform when the conference was underway the following week. She had the beginnings of a headache – lecture theatres with no natural light always had that effect – making it hard to concentrate. Besides ... it was disconcerting to be daydreaming about the chaplain, willing sessions to end so she could check her phone for text messages, at a professional event of this importance.

She forced herself to attend more closely. *Get thee behind me, Ruaidhri.* There were always additional sensitivities and pitfalls with an international audience; you had to be aware of agendas below the surface, cultural norms that weren't always spelled out. And this was a lively forum, the questions coming thick and fast after each paper. She concentrated on the other speakers, consultants and researchers, who seemed to have no trouble fielding each comment adroitly. If only she could be that articulate.

'And now,' the chairman announced, 'Sarah Jenkins, Senior Nurse in Organ Donation here in Edinburgh, will tell us more about the problems of recruiting donors in the UK.'

She was confident her talk was well structured, and she'd prepared thoroughly, so that part in the spotlight at least held no fears.

'Other countries have already implemented presumed consent instead of opting-in.' The woman with fabulous black hair and film star looks was waving her hand with the first question as soon as Sarah stopped speaking.

'Yes, indeed – Austria, Belgium, France, Singapore, Sweden, Spain.' Sarah nodded.

'In my country, Spain, it has increased the numbers significantly,' the woman said. 'Could the UK learn from our experience?'

'Well, I think a significant factor in your improved rates is the huge investment your countries have made in this area, and the massive programmes implemented to educate the public. I wish we had more resources to do something similar here.' Ruaidhri's voice – *Try to make 'em laugh; I reckon if they laugh with you you've got them on your side* – rang somewhere in the back of her mind. 'But I'd add a wee caveat. My colleagues would be utterly staggered to hear what I'm about to say next. I'm pathologically allergic to statistics.' She shivered in an exaggerated way and noted the responsive smiles. 'So I shall need a massive dose of anti-histamines as soon as I leave this platform. But if you look at the figures carefully, I think you'll find that it's all relative. For example, even in spite of a major investment and introducing opting-out, Sweden's donation rate is still lower than ours in the UK. And for you in Spain, yes, your figures are improving under the new system, but it's taken eleven years and a big expensive recruitment drive to get where you've got today.'

Before the Spanish delegate could reply, the chairman invited a black man with a shining bald head to ask his question.

'What steps would you recommend to increase uptake apart from education?'

I'd have guys dressed up like livers and hearts and kidneys cornering folk in the street ...

'I'd adopt a multi-pronged approach. When you go to the GP, he treats your irritable bowel or your infected toenail, but he also asks if you've considered joining the organ donation register. You go to your lawyer to draw up your will; he includes bequeathing your organs alongside your house and your stamp collection and your great-granny's diamond tiara. You go to your local supermarket and the forms are there too alongside your 25p-off vouchers and your 3-for-2 offers. Your kids go off to school and in their biology class, as well as the structure of the heart, they learn that second-hand hearts are really valuable. Likewise in Religion and Moral Philosophy – or whatever the subject's called nowadays – you include the ethics of organ donation. I think it's about raising awareness across the board.'

'I think we need to send you along to talk to the MSPs,' laughed the chairman.

Thanks, Ruaidhri.

But the next delegate drove the smile from her face and Ruaidhri from her mind. She was a young Indian-looking woman whose voice quivered with emotion as she described the horror of watching her sister die waiting for a heart. She wanted to know what Sarah would do to prevent such a waste of life. In these emergencies you couldn't wait for the longer-term strategies to take effect, the woman said, you needed solutions now.

Sarah was instantly back in her everyday role. 'I'm so sorry to hear about your sister. Without knowing the clinical detail I can't say for sure what I'd do in that case, but I totally understand your frustration and sadness. I think perhaps we've become so obsessed with the ideal that we've overlooked the potential for resorting to the less-than-optimal in extreme circumstances. Sometimes if the situation is desperate, maybe there's a case for using non-beating hearts, a sort of holding exercise. That might be preferable to running out of time waiting for that perfect heart to become available. But there are other implications, and anyway you might feel differently. Would you have been happy with second-best for your sister? I don't know.'

The woman shrugged.

Sarah was on the point of adding something about the shortage of donors from certain ethnic minority groups, but stopped herself. Who knew what racial sensitivities or superstitions and cultural norms this grieving sister espoused herself?

Another delegate was waving a programme in the air. He didn't wait for the microphone or chairman's permission.

'You mentioned teaching kids in their Moral Philosophy classes, but what about religious objections? Some people do have strong issues with these things. How would you change that?'

Ruaidhri, where are you?

'In my experience you can't do much to change religious scruples. If you believe something, you believe it. And if it's about very deep-seated conviction, and your relationship with God, and hope of an afterlife, and all that sort of thing, I wouldn't personally want to undermine someone's faith, especially when they're at their most vulnerable.'

'One last question?' the chairman said.

'What about the safety aspects of an opt-out system?' The question came from a portly man on the front row who looked vaguely familiar, but Sarah couldn't quite place him.

'Good point,' she said with a smile. 'For me the biggest issue there is the two hours or so of detailed questioning we currently go through when obtaining authorisation – taking behavioural, medical, sexual histories. At the moment the families participate willingly, but with an opt-out system this could be compromised and potentially jeopardise safety.'

The questioner nodded but before he could reply the chairman intervened. Sarah's time was up.

Could the Beacham's problem have been religious objection? Sxx, she texted in the tea break.

Don't think so. More about something in E's past, I thought. Rxx, Ruaidhri replied.

'What made you think it was about Elvira's history?' she asked him the following afternoon in her office. 'Nothing came up in the screening.'

'Well, Mrs Beacham was very hung up on Elvira's secret thoughts, didn't want them passed on. My guess is there was something in the past that her mum didn't want anybody else to know.'

'Strange. Her dad was more hung up on how deserving the *recipient* was, not Elvira.'

'Well, it worked out right in the end, whoever pressed the right buttons,' he said with a smile.

She shrugged. 'Still bugs me though. I hope we supported them enough.'

'So,' he said briskly, 'happy with your slot yesterday at the conference?'

'So-so. I think I made a mess of a religious scruples question.' She outlined the exchange. 'What would you have said?'

'I agree with you up to a point, nothing to gain by rocking somebody's faith. But I'd personally sometimes challenge the person gently if I think their position is one of ignorance or brain washing or prejudice, and if their rigid view isn't helping their present situation.'

'That's a better answer.'

'No, it's *my* answer. Yours is perfectly fair for someone with your nursing background and responsibility for supporting them holistically. You can get hauled over the coals for talking about religion, can't you?'

'Indeed we can.'

'Yes. Whereas it's a bona fide part of my job.'

Sarah sighed. 'It's so hard for these families. You don't want to knock any of their props from under them.'

'Absolutely. All I can say is, I hope you're around if I'm ever in a situation where I need to weigh up the pros and cons myself.'

'Happy to oblige.'

'Although, on second thoughts, I'd rather have you … no, I'm not allowed to say that here. It'd be over-stepping the boundary between reassuringly professional, and excitingly intimate.' His expression had already exceeded those limits.

'I'll tell you where I'd like you to be some other time, when you're not sitting at arms length, wearing that do-not-touch look.'

Sarah laughed out loud. 'You're incorrigible.'

'But sticking very properly to the rules of engagement, grant me that. Have you any idea how hard it is to resist temptation here? Couldn't you possibly knock off duty for a break earlier than 7pm?'

'Depends how quickly I get through this backlog of correspondence, and whatever else comes into ICU or the ED today. And how many interruptions I get.'

'Fair enough. So I'd better be off now before I infringe your notion of propriety, set tongues wagging, and put my cause back a month.'

She put out a hand and let it rest on his arm. 'Thanks for dropping in, Ruaidhri. And for what it's worth, I'm sorely tempted to break the rules too, but ...' she shrugged. 'Where would it end?'

'Where indeed.'

Before she knew what he intended Ruaidhri stooped and kissed her. 'Till tonight.' And he was gone.

Chapter 35

Carole

'I'M BACK, ELLIE. Your dad wasn't keen on me coming today, but I had to. Usually I try not to let him know if I'm feeling weepy, but the letter caught me by surprise. It brought everything back with a vengeance, and the tears just came.

'He knew about the letter, this one about the eyes, I mean. He read it before I did. He's taken to reading the post first these days, reckons he needs to protect me from the emotion of it all. And I see what he means; some days I do cope better than others. I hope he isn't keeping stuff back from me about you, though, and the folk who've got your organs, and everything. But there again, do I want to know if things go wrong? I don't know. Maybe not. I caught him shredding one letter the other day, but he insisted it was just something from a crank, not worth bothering about.

'Anyway, I told him, "OK, I am upset, but I still need to go to the grave." I don't think he understands. Talking to you is the one thing that really helps. You won't worry if I weep and sniffle a bit, and I'll feel better for sharing it with you.

'You see, letting them have your eyes was the bit that I really had the hardest time with. It's not rational, I know, but there's something about eyes – they're a window to the soul. They tell you so much about the person. And you had such beautiful eyes, Ellie. Unusual, dark hazel, like your grandmother. You were so like her in lots of ways. Oh, I know, of course, they only use the clear bit at the front, not the whole eye, not even the iris where the colour is, but still.

'So getting the letter today brought back all that agonising. Now I know for sure somebody else, well, two people actually, are walking round looking through your eyes, and … it makes me cry. It should be you.

'I'll read you what it says:

… your daughter's corneas went to a young woman in Newcastle and an older woman in Dumfries.

The gift of sight is a very precious thing to give and I'm pleased to say that both these women are doing really well. I enclose letters from both of them. As a woman yourself I'm sure you will empathise with the joy they find in being able to apply their make-up and see their loved ones clearly again.

'I'll let you know what they say themselves in a minute, but first I need to … get a grip … think about … something else … Sorry. How pathetic am I?

'In fact, why don't I tell you what I found out? I figured concentrating on the medical aspects might make it all seem less emotional, help me to focus on the mechanical, positive side. Did you do any research, I wonder, maybe even visit the same sites? Sorry if you know all this already.

'Did you know, for instance, that corneas are the most common and successful of all transplants? I didn't. Ninety per cent success rate. Pretty good, huh? What's not to like? And so many folk need them. Once the smoothness and clarity of that transparent film is lost – through disease or trauma or whatever – the light gets distorted and you get reduced vision or glare or whatever, and so, getting perfect replacements counts for a lot.

'I'm going to check out if I can donate my eyes too. I presume the cancer will rule out some stuff, but the eyes – maybe they'll still be useable. I can ask anyway.

'There, I think I'm OK again now.

'This card's from the lady in Dumfries, Margaret R – bit

like royalty, eh? Elizabeth R. Margaret R. Perhaps that's why she does it. Anyway, it's a calla lily against a black background, and inside it says, Thinking of you. *And this lady, Margaret R, writes:*

I'm feeling hopelessly not up to the task of writing this card.

If anything happened to one of my children I don't think I could cope. But you found the strength to let them have your daughter's organs. In my book that deserves an OBE – much more so than these celebrities, sports people or actresses or TV folk.

You won't want to know the details but I'd got to the stage of being registered, needing all sorts of aids from the RNIB. Now I can do pretty much everything I want to do. I have to keep pinching myself just to be sure it isn't a dream and I'm going to wake up and be incredibly disappointed.

Music is my first love and now I can actually see the music again. I can even see the score well enough to try new pieces – piano and violin. I can't tell you what that means to me.

I know it's a wee extra luxury when you put it against the loss of your daughter's life, but I imagine you donated other organs to literally save lives as well. Giving me back my sight is one more good thing you did. And I'm so grateful.

I've written this by hand – sorry about the scrappy writing, but I wanted to show you what I can do now, I couldn't even sign my name in a straight line before.

I hope you get your reward.

'She signs herself **Margaret R** *and adds in brackets* **They tell you not to put your full name, sorry.** *We know that, of course, but I guess it felt odd for her.*

'She sounds nice though, doesn't she?

'And here's the letter from the young woman in Newcastle. Her name's … I think it's Fallon. People often sign their name in a kind of slapdash fashion, don't they? The rest of it is typed so it's perfectly legible.

Dear wonderful people

I wonder if you've ever had difficulty seeing the number on a bus, reading the timetable, applying your make-up, finding a dropped pill or stitch, or pouring hot water into a mug.

But thanks to your daughter I can now do all these things again. And I can help my children with their schoolwork, drive the car, write the Christmas cards – oh, so many things I thought were gone for good. They might seem trivial to you, but believe me when you've faced going completely blind, being able to see clearly again is a miracle. Especially for a young mum with small children to care for.

So I want to say a great big thank you for giving me back my sight, surely one of the most precious gifts anybody could ever give. I'm desperately sorry your daughter died but I hope it comforts you to know she helped so many other people.

All best

Fallon

'See what a difference you've made, Ellie. Isn't that lovely. And it does help, seeing it from her side. If you'd been

the one going blind I'd have wanted some other family to help you.

'But I must tell you something else about this lady in Newcastle – sort of anyway. Something spooky and ... well, see what you think.

'Oliver came yesterday. He's changed. He's much more relaxed with us, and ... I don't know, softer, warmer. I'm starting to see why you fell for him. But this time he told me something really weird.

'He was in a restaurant down in Newcastle. With a female colleague – nothing more than business he said – a bit too quickly, I thought, but it's his life, none of my concern. If he's moving on that's his affair. I thought actually he was rather keen on Sarah – you know, the transplant nurse who helped us. He seemed pretty smitten, but he says it was only that he was impressed by her skill and compassion. Besides he reckons she's got a thing going with the chaplain. Mr Cameron was lovely to us when you had the accident, so I hope it's true. They're both exceptionally caring, lovely people, a winning team, although how they ever get time to see each other I can't imagine. They both seem to spend all the hours God sends at the hospital, day and night.

'Anyway ... what was I saying? I do ramble on when I come to see you. Sorry. At least you aren't embarrassed by me now. Ah yes, Oliver. He was in this restaurant and there was a lady sitting in the corner waiting. She was wearing dark glasses, but he said he could feel her staring at him. After a bit he went over and said, "Sorry, but do I know you?" She didn't say anything at first but slowly took off her glasses and looked up at him. And then she said, "I rather think you might do."

'He said it was really freaky. She had your eyes. It really shook him. He mumbled something non-committal, and hightailed it out of there. He was shaking. After a bit he went back in, but the woman had gone, and his colleague was totally mystified and not in the least bit pleased about being left high and dry, so he paid the bill and they left.

'But then he started to think more about it and was kicking himself because he hadn't at least asked the woman if she'd had a corneal transplant. The odd thing is, Ellie, this

letter from Fallon hadn't even arrived, so he couldn't have known there was somebody in Newcastle with your cornea. It wasn't in his subconscious or anything.

'I can think of all sorts of things against it being that same person. She'd still have had her eyes shielded this close to the operation, wouldn't she? Or was she using the dark glasses instead? But it's spooky, don't you think? Imagine if her eyes – your cornea – did recognise him. No, that's nonsense.

'But you must admit, it's odd.

'Oliver reckons he generally keeps the past locked away inside nowadays. If anybody asks, he just says he had someone special; she was killed; he's moving on. Fair enough, if it helps him cope. But he did admit he still gets nightmares, about the accident, and the transplants.

'I don't any more, so, by way of reassurance, I told him that I'd come full circle. I want to be a donor myself, and the corneas are one thing they can use irrespective of age so I want them to take mine.

'And I said, if he was still haunted by this woman, why not contact Sarah, talk to her about it. She'd know more if there was any possibility it could be the same person. But he wasn't keen on that idea. Doesn't want to make a fool of himself, he says, not in front of her. I guess I can sort of see why. Specially if he does still carry a torch for her.

'But you know, afterwards, I looked it up and it seems heaps of people do believe in cellular memory. Mr Cameron convinced me it couldn't be true and I kind of believe him, but there are loads of stories that don't have a rational explanation. I really, really, really don't want it to be true in your case, don't want anybody else knowing your secrets and your past.

'Goodness, what a fuss and palaver over two little bits of transparent tissue. Imagine if they'd taken your face! But that's terribly rare, mercifully. I can remember the first one – a partial face in 2005 in France. You can understand the need, but the face! Makes me shudder to think about it. Think of all the big psychological issues attached to your face. It's like your whole identity. Sacred in some way. Imagine what would happen if somebody rejected a face.

'*At least afterwards you still looked like you. That's a comfort. Heavens! Look at the time. I must get back. Sorry to warble on, Ellie. I'll be back tomorrow.*'

Chapter 36

Elvira's corneas

THE SHRILL RINGING of the phone woke her.

'Hilary Donaldson speaking.'

'Hi, Hils.'

'Hi, yourself.'

'Busy?'

'Nope.'

'See you then.'

'OK.'

Hilary tumbled out of bed. Their particular brand of twin-speak sounded terse to others, but she knew exactly how her sister, Fallon, was feeling. She glanced at the clock. Damn, she'd have to call a taxi. If she couldn't read a clock-face today she wouldn't be fit to cycle.

Fumbling for her clothes she inwardly cursed her inheritance – their joint inheritance: Fuch's endothelial dystrophy.

The consultant had been so confident: 'You needn't start expecting any significant loss of vision until you're in your fifties, maybe even sixties.' And he waffled on about various homely tactics they might adopt involving things like hairdryers blowing across the face, drying out the corneas. How she and Fallon had laughed at the pictures it conjured up. The caveat trailed along almost as an afterthought: '… as long as you avoid trauma or infection.' Well, no sweat there, they'd both be extra careful. Sight was so precious.

They'd relaxed.

Fallon hadn't even been thinking 'danger' when she'd released the kitchen blind that morning. Far from it; she'd been simultaneously leaning forward to smell the roses on the window-sill when the cord flipped towards her with that lethal plastic disc on the end. It caught her just as the sun streamed into the room, temporarily blinding her, cutting into an eye already oedematous and thickened by disease. Five weeks later the blisters had her weeping in agony, and the 'temporary' threatened to become 'permanent'.

Hilary had gone home and beaten the daylights out of her rugs the day Fallon was told there was only one option left – a transplant. Why did it have to happen to her beloved twin? They'd only just celebrated their thirty-ninth birthday.

See, that was the thing with identical twins. Hilary could watch her own future being played out in front of her. She'd already rehearsed the pain, the restrictions, the frustration. Not only because she was following on behind – same genes, same disease – but because they shared much much more than a birthday.

The twins were eight before anybody else realised they had a remarkable connection.

Hilary was away on a class trip to an adventure centre, but her twin had insisted, 'Hils is poorly, Mummy. Really really poorly.' Her mother got annoyed by her persistent wailing as she rocked herself in a fetal curl, clutching her tummy. She lectured the child on the evils of attention-seeking and fantasizing. When the call came telling her that Hilary had been taken to hospital with appendicitis, Mrs Dawson gave her well daughter a worried look.

When Hilary anticipated Fallon's late arrival at a swimming competition, and knew she'd missed the bus, the twins themselves felt a shiver down their spines.

By the time they were twelve and Hilary complained of a terrible headache, it was their mother who begged the doctors to do tests on Fallon. When the lumbar puncture showed she was the one with meningitis, everyone looked at both girls strangely. They heard the words bandied about in subdued whispers, 'freaky', 'weird', 'scary'.

When they both confessed to blurred vision in the mornings neither of them knew who actually had the problem. They exchanged stories – dropping stitches in their knitting ... misjudging the edge of a mug, pouring hot water over the table ... not being able to see the number on a bus ... fouling up recipes ... making a dog's breakfast of their make-up. Their families bore out their accounts. The children ridiculed their mothers' clumsiness equating it to advancing age. Their husbands picked up the slack whenever they could, both hanging on to the forlorn hope that the problems in their case were fantastically sympathetic.

But the ophthalmic specialists agreed – both had an inherited disorder; both were on a pathway to blindness.

After the incident with the kitchen blind Fallon's disease raced away ahead of Hilary's. She started falling, having accidents, and her husband worried he'd be under suspicion for domestic abuse. He couldn't kid himself any longer. Nobody could.

Fallon opened the door on her first ring. They held each other tightly, letting the sympathy flow.

'How's it going?' Hilary asked her.

'Healing nicely since the stitches came out,' Fallon said. 'Weird though, knowing I'm seeing through somebody else's eye.'

'Consultant happy?'

'Yep. Reckons I needn't go back for another month.'

'Excellent. Is he nice?'

'Lovely. Pretty dishy too! Just as well since I'm going to be seeing him every month for a bit. And at least once a year for the rest of my long-legged life, huh?'

'I love the new specs,' Hilary said. 'Very snazzy.'

'Yours new too?'

'Yep. Strong tint all the time, and stronger photosensitive bit. Cuts down the glare more. Did you find that difficult?'

'Yep.'

'Funny though, I had a weird experience first time I wore them on Monday. I was having a bit of a bad day anyway, everything very blurry, but I kept them on. Felt more comfortable with the light reduced. I was meeting a pal in the afternoon so I popped into this restaurant for a bite of lunch. I was experimenting looking at things to see how long it took to get a clear view when this guy comes up to me.

'"Sorry, but do I know you?" he says.

'I could see he was dark, and about forty, and he had on a really white shirt, but that was about it. And I didn't recognise the voice. Taking off the glasses didn't help either. I tried to focus on his face and I said something daft like, "I rather think you might do," just to buy a bit of time, give me space to listen to what he said, pick up cues, fall in with his conversation as soon as I'd got my compass.

'The guy stared for a minute – I could see him better by that time – and then he looked as if he'd seen a ghost. He shot out of that restaurant like a bat out of hell. I checked in the mirror afterwards but there wasn't anything strange about my make-up or anything, so I guess he must have been a weirdo. Unless … d'you know anybody answering that description? Did he mistake me for you?'

'Dark, in his forties, white shirt? Could be a dozen guys I know. But none of them would belt out of the place as soon as they looked into my eyes. Or your eyes.'

'Fair enough. Lunatic fringe then.'

'Seems like it. That why you called me?'

'Partly. But more importantly, to tell you to go and see your consultant. Feels bad, Hils. Get things checked out. I reckon your condition's speeded up.'

'Damn. You sure?'

'Not hundred percent but it's like the other times.'

'Scunners.'

'I can recommend a transplant.'

Chapter 37

Carole

'ELLIE, I'M AFRAID I'm going to have to ease off from visiting you. Things are moving pretty fast now. The drugs keep the pain manageable most of the time but my bones are weakening and it's hard to get around.

'Dad says he'll bring me in a wheelchair if I want to come again. I might do, but I'm not sure I'll be able, and anyway I couldn't talk to you like I do if anybody else was here. So I want to say a few things just in case this is my last chance. Dad's coming back to collect me soon. He says there's no point in hastening my end by getting chilled up here; you wouldn't want that. He's probably right, although I don't want this last stage to go on and on. A nice little dose of pneumonia might be just the ticket.

'The boys are up at the moment. Lovely to see them again. And I'm pretty sure they'll be along to visit you later. I suspect Dad told them I wasn't so good, bless him, but I don't want them worrying about me, they've got their own lives to lead.

'So, where was I? Goodness, my mind's so wandery these days.

'Ah, yes. The first thing is, I owe you an apology. For all those years that I didn't quite trust you, worried that there was still something fierce and wild lurking below the surface, the something that killed Sally. But the sympathy letters, the things people have told me, they've shown me that you were better than the person I saw. You were always doing kind acts, *and you did it all without fanfare. We had no idea of the extent of your caring. I am so, so sorry I ever doubted you. You were only a child back then, a confused child, not an evil monster. If anyone was to blame it was me. Did you sense my distrust? Were you just fighting against my controlling ways?*

'I'm so glad that bits of you and Maddie live on, giving a life to all those other people. What a legacy.

'Next thing, I want you to know that Dad and I are going to stay together. Not long now. If you hadn't died I wouldn't have stayed with him. You know that. I didn't know he knew, *though.'*

Guy swung round to face her directly.

'Of course I knew,' he said.

'Why "of course"?'

He threw her that look that always seemed to imply disbelief at her stupidity. 'Because I've known you for nigh on half a century, maybe.'

'So why didn't you say something?'

'If I'd put in my tuppence worth, or tried to persuade you, you'd have dug your heels in even harder. You'd have resented my "interference", my "controlling" you.'

'Didn't you care if I went?'

'Of course I cared – too much to risk pushing you further away. I can't imagine life without you. Besides who else would put up with me? I thought if I sat tight you'd come back. We've become a habit, you and me, not easy to break.'

A habit. Hmm ... not very romantic, but it was more honest than something flowery.

'Who'd put up with me, *is more the issue. But of course your dad doesn't say that. He never does. And perversely I don't think he even thinks it. He's never been one to criticise or try to change me.*

'I don't know, Ellie. If you hadn't died, would I have had the courage to make the break? Would I have been happier on my own? We'll never know.

'We're all grieving, all struggling, thrown together out of necessity. But then, sharing responsibility for Willow, both of us caring, we've changed somehow, subtly, changed into something warmer. We laugh together again, we even cry together sometimes. It's like a second chance. And we both want to do better this time round. We've achieved a kind of peace.

'Maybe it helps knowing we don't have much time left. We can surely manage a kind of truce for a few weeks. Maybe not years and years, but weeks, yes.

'Of course, I don't paint any more. No time. No inclination either. I hate the room, the easel, the brushes – they remind me too much of that terrible day when the police came. I'm glad that the last proper thing I did was your picture, and you've got that, so I don't even have to look at it and worry that it wasn't good enough for you. As I rolled it up, it was like gathering together all those thoughts of you that I had while I was doing it, sealing them inside it, to lie snugly beside you for ever.

'What else is there? Oh yes. Dad. He's doing more and more in the house – I haven't got the stamina now. And he's surprisingly good in the kitchen, you know, and in the garden. I guess he never had a chance to show what he could do when I kept it all to myself.

'And the last thing I have to tell you – guess what? All this time I've been wondering who was visiting you, bringing flowers. At first I was scared. Was it someone taunting me, telling me he knew our secret? Then, when nothing bad happened, I thought maybe you had a secret admirer. I felt so jealous that someone else got it so right. Like with the violets, and that gorgeous Christmas wreath. Well, you do have an admirer.

'Your father.

'I thought he was totally unsentimental about graves and things. Turns out he isn't. He says he doesn't talk to you, but he sits here and thinks about you both, and sometimes he cries. I'd never seen him cry before we lost you, not even when Sally died. Something just closed off in him then. He's always seemed so untouchable, so imperturbable.

'And apparently once a year – on her birthday – he orders a wreath to be put on Sally's grave. Thirty-one times he's done that now, and I never even knew. If you'd asked me, I'd have said he'd probably forgotten the date altogether. But no. Just shows you how wrong you can be about somebody you think you know inside out.

'I guess I've been the selfish one. I wanted to put a distance between us and the whole Sally-business, protect the rest of us from the fallout. I was so wrapped up in my loss, my need, I didn't notice how vulnerable he was. I like him more with wavy edges, I like knowing that he hurts too, that he cares, and I'm glad Willow will have him when I've gone. He's the next best thing to you she could have. Much, much better than me.

'Ahh, here he comes now. Oh, and Freddie and Kenyon are with him. Isn't that lovely? All of us together, one last time.

'Bye, my darling. See you soon.'

Over My Dead Body

Discussion Points for Bookclubs

- What are the main characteristics you would attribute to Elvira, Carole, Guy and Willow? How far do you think these account for the tensions within the family?

- We hear a lot about Carole's feelings and opinions. How accurate do you think her perceptions of a) herself, b) her husband and c) her daughter are? Did your opinion of Guy change by the end of the book?

- Why do you think Carole is so obsessed by what happened to Sally? Are her fears about a) Elvira, b) the organs, and c) Willow justified? What was your response to the revelation?

- The policeman, Lennox McRobert, has confidential information from the past. Was he justified in a) reassuring Carole, b) not sharing it with the Family Liaison Officer?

- Carole takes steps to protect Elvira's memory (an isolated grave, a simple headstone, withdrawing her book of poems). Does this behaviour tally with your picture of her? How does it square with her replying to the letter of thanks Sam sent?

- In Chapter 18 Carole lists a number of reasons why she doesn't want to donate Elvira's organs. How far do you a) sympathise with her reservations, b) agree with her final decision, c) feel she was influenced by Oliver or the chaplain?

- Has this book changed your personal opinions about organ donation? Are there any circumstances which would make you say no to either receiving or donating an organ? Are there any organs or tissues you would personally not want used from a) yourself or b) your child?

- Oliver asks: *'What's the point of deciding for yourself, carrying a card, being on the register and everything, if they don't take any notice when you're dead?'* How would you answer him? Of all those connected to Elvira, whose opinions about the use of her organs should carry most weight? Why?

- Several people in this story are exercised by the 'worthiness' of potential recipients and their unhealthy lifestyles. The specialist nurses assure them that decisions are made on the basis of medical need, by impartial assessors and computers. What are your opinions on this? Does hearing the recipients' stories influence your views about the use of Elvira and Madeline's organs?

- Would you support the use of organs from a) impoverished foreigners, b) executed prisoners?

- Patty Ingram wanted to give her own kidney to her brother, Sam. He refused it. What do you think about live donation a) to a relative, b) to a stranger, and c) through a chain of patients and their relatives?

- There is a shortage of organs available for transplantation. Far more people agree with organ donation than sign the donor register. Which of the steps to encourage participation listed in Chapter 34 did you find most persuasive? Can you think of any others?

- Sometimes transplanted organs fail or are rejected. Sarah wonders if donor families should be told. Would you wish to know?

- How appropriate do you think it is for a recipient to a) want to name a baby after the donor, b) send before-and-after photos of himself to the donor's family, c) try to discover the identity of the donor, and d) contact the donor's family?

- What do you think about the role letters play in this book? What characteristics would you suggest make up the ideal letter from recipient to donor family?

If you are interested in further information about medical ethics or this series of books, visit the author's website which provides further discussion points for students and teachers on ethical issues; an author profile; links to related websites; and a weekly blog.

www.hazelmchaffie.com

By the same author

Saving Sebastian
ISBN 978 1 906817 87 9   PBK and eBook

Sebastian Zair is four years old, but a rare blood disorder means that he won't live much longer unless he gets a stem cell transplant.

His mother is determined to save him. With no one in the family a match, she appeals to the Pemberton Fertility Centre for help to create an embryo the same tissue type as Sebastian.

But will her resolve falter as her fortieth birthday approaches? When hormones play havoc with her confidence and control? When the Pemberton becomes the focus of a major inquiry following the birth of a white baby to black parents? When an unscrupulous journalist starts to invade the family's privacy? When militant pro-life campaigners protest against the wanton destruction of life?

It's a race against time, and time is not on Sebastian's side.

Remember Remember
ISBN 978 1906817 78 7   PBK

Doris Mannering's secret has been safely kept for 60 years, but now it's threatened with exposure.

In her early twenties during World War II she made a choice that changed the course of her family's life. The evidence was safely buried, but now, with the onset of Alzheimer's, her mind is wandering. She is haunted by the feeling that she must find the papers before it's too late, but she just can't remember ...

Jessica is driven to despair by her mother's behaviour, but it's not until lives are in jeopardy that she consents to Doris going into a residential home. As she begins clearing the family home ready for sale, bittersweet memories and unexpected discoveries await her. But these pale into insignificance against the bombshell her lawyer lover, Aaron, hands her.

Right to Die
ISBN 1 906307 21 0   PBK

Naomi is haunted by a troubling secret. Struggling to come to terms with her husband's death, her biggest dread is finding out that Adam knew of her betrayal. He left behind an intimate diary – but dare she read it? Will it set her mind at ease – or will it destroy the fragile hold she has over her grief?

Gripped by his unfolding story, Naomi discovers more than she bargained for. Adam writes of his feelings for her, his career, his burning ambition. How his dreams evaporate when he is diagnosed with Motor Neurone Disease, as one by one he loses the ability to walk, to speak, to swallow. How he resolves to mastermind his own exit at a time of his choosing ... but time is one luxury he can't afford. Can he, will he, ask a friend, or even a relative, to help him die?

Vacant Possession
ISBN 1 85775 651 7   PBK and eBook

Following a serious accident, Vivienne Faraday has been in a persistent vegetative state, looked after in a residential home, for years. How can she suddenly be pregnant?

She can't speak for herself so who should decide what happens to the unborn child? Who knows what's in her best interests? Her father, her brothers, her estranged mother who is now a nun, the medical director, the police, all have different opinions as to the best way forward. They also have their personal interests and values.

As events gather momentum, and the baby grows, someone must make medical and moral choices on Vivienne's behalf, choices beset with uncertainty, which profoundly affect their own relationships and futures. And all the time suspicion mounts: who exactly is the rapist?

Paternity
ISBN 1 85775 652 5   PBK and eBook

When Judy agrees to marry Declan Robertson his happiness knows no bounds. But from the very first night of their marriage cracks appear in their relationship, which only widen until Judy finally reveals the demons that haunt her.

Then tragedy strikes, threatening their new security: a child dies. Questions follow, questions that rock their foundations to the core. A history of deception and half-truths masquerading as love begins to unravel, challenging their very identities. Who are they? What have they inherited? What are they passing on to future generations? Do they have a future together?

Declan has always lived by a strict moral code; now he must ask himself just how far he will go to protect his wife from the consequences of her parent's actions.

Double Trouble
ISBN 1 85775 669 X   PBK and eBook

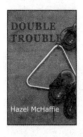

The Halleys are a close-knit, successful, loving family. Relationships become strained when identical twins. Michael and Nicholas, fall in love with the same girl, Donella, herself a twin. On the rebound from Nick, Donella eventually marries Mike, but their lives become entangled again when Nick returns from work overseas. His new wife, Heidi, is Swiss, reserved, and haunted by her past; she finds it difficult to find her niche within the demonstrative Halley family.

But Donella's three daughters gradually break down the barriers and a new order is established. Later, when Heidi finds she can't have children of her own, new tensions emerge. Fresh alliances are forged; old feelings return; jealousies develop; mental illness and a surrogate pregnancy threaten the delicate peace the couples have established. Will the family survive intact?